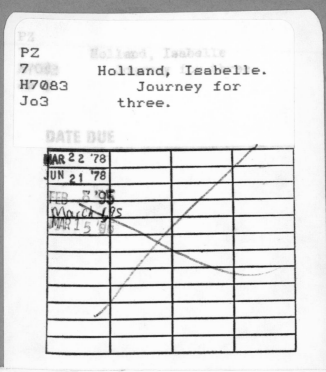

LENDING POLICY

IF YOU DAMAGE OR LOSE LIBRARY
MATERIALS, THEN YOU WILL BE
CHARGED FOR REPLACEMENT. FAIL-
URE TO PAY AFFECTS LIBRARY
PRIVILEGES, GRADES, TRANSCRIPTS,
DIPLOMAS, AND REGISTRATION
PRIVILEGES OR ANY COMBINATION
THEREOF.

Journey for Three

Journey for Three

by Isabelle Holland

illustrated by Charles Robinson

HOUGHTON MIFFLIN COMPANY BOSTON

Library of Congress Cataloging in Publication Data

Holland, Isabelle.
  Journey for three.
                            contents
  SUMMARY: Alison, a spunky eleven-year-old orphan,
finds a home for herself and her two younger "brothers"
with a reluctant bachelor uncle.
  [1. Orphans--Fiction] I. Robinson, Charles,
1931-   illus. II. Title.
PZ7.H7083Jo3   [Fic]   74-17382
ISBN 0-395-20213-2

This edition published by Houghton Mifflin Company
by arrangement with Xerox Weekly Reader Family Books,
Middletown, Connecticut.

For Isabel and Phoebe

1

"Well, there's the house, or at least there's a sign," the driver of the truck said. "But I don't feel right about letting you out here. Are you sure you don't want me to take you back to town?"

"No, thank you," Alison Cairn said, firmly opening the door on her side and jumping down onto the road.

The driver got out and took her suitcase over to her. A big man, he towered over the little girl.

"How old are you?" he asked almost accusingly.

"Eleven. Going on twelve."

"How much going on?"

Alison sighed. "I was eleven last month."

"I thought so. You say he's your Uncle Nicholas?"

"Well, actually, he's my father's cousin, so that makes him my second cousin. But he's my closest surviving relative" — she said it as though she were reciting a well-learned line — "so therefore I'm going to live with him."

"Does he know you're coming?"

"Of course. Mrs. Daniels wrote to him." She looked at the big truckman a little anxiously. "I told you about Mrs. Daniels at the mission?"

"Yeah. You sure been around. Where did you say that mission was?"

"Lots of places: India, South America, everywhere. But I have to go now. Thank you very much. Goodbye."

And before the truck driver could reply, she was hopping over the green turf onto a path that curved around a small hill, her thin legs moving swiftly. At the point where the path curved, she turned and waved.

The man waved back. Then she was gone. He stared across the vista of grass and gray rocks to the sea beyond. There was a puzzled look on his kindly face. "I guess it's all right," he said to himself. He took another look at the sign. It was simply a rough wooden plank with the words "Four Winds" painted on it in white. Beside the sign was a covered mail box on which was also painted "Four Winds" and underneath that, "Nicholas Mac-Bain."

It was a long way to the house. The path ran up and down parallel to the shoreline below and then veered east with the headland that stuck out into the sea. The suitcase was heavy and Alison's shoes were thin and worn. But there was a determined look on her small, sallow face. Although the thin soles of her shoes occasionally slipped on small rocks, and she had to change the suitcase from hand to hand, she finally arrived within sight of the house.

It was rather ugly, with no special shape, and unpainted. It sat baldy on the crest of the headland, unprotected by the spruce and fir and pine that lay further back. There were one or two isolated trees around it, gnarled and bent. It was bleak and looked inhospitable. But Alison's face, as she stared at it from about a hundred yards away, smoothed into a smile.

"It's okay," she said to herself. "It'll be just fine."

She finally got to the front door by the narrow, rocky road that led up to it, with a side branch off to what looked like a barn or shed. She couldn't see that there were any lights on, but there was smoke coming out the chimney. This reassured her, although, as she crossed the last five yards to the front door, she realized that did not necessarily mean her Uncle Nicholas was home. There was no bell. But there was a knocker shaped like an anchor, so she stood on tiptoe and gave it a sharp rat-tat-tat-tat.

It seemed like a long wait, and she was about to rap again when the door appeared to fling itself open. The man that stood there was large and dark with black hair and beard and was wearing a black sweater and faded blue jeans. He seemed to loom over her. "What do you want?" he asked.

Alison stared up into that unwelcoming face with its snapped together mouth and her courage quailed. But she remembered everything the village holy man back at the mission in India had said and concentrated on imagining her Uncle Nicholas with a warm smile and words something like, "You must be my niece Alison!

How glad I am to see you! Do come in!" It took a great deal of imagination. Fortunately, Alison had a great deal, and it was taking all she had because the man was not cooperating. He was saying in an exasperated voice, "I asked you what you wanted."

Alison fixed her gaze on his imagined smile and said, "I'm your niece, or at least your cousin, Alison Cairn. I've come to live with you."

Nicholas MacBain looked stunned for a moment. Then he looked furious. Then he said, "Oh, no, you're not."

"Didn't you get Mrs. Daniels' letter from the mission?"

"I got a letter from a silly woman half way across the world at some address I couldn't read, as I couldn't read half of her letter."

"She doesn't like the typewriter," Alison explained. "The letter said since my parents were dead and the mission was being closed and you were one of my last surviving relatives, could I come and live with you?"

"Well, you can't. I'm a bachelor and I live alone. Furthermore, I don't like children or females and you're both. You're going to have to go back."

"I'm not going back," Alison said.

"You must have some other relatives."

Alison caught the "other." She said, "At least you admit I am related to you. It was through my father's mother, who was named MacBain."

"I don't care who it was through. You're not coming here. I'm a hermit, a recluse."

"Like St. Anthony?" Alison asked, thinking perhaps they had found a bond.

"No. Not like St. Anthony or any other saint. I'm a

writer. I need solitude. And besides, I told you. I don't
like children."

Alison stared at his face and then down at her toes.
She was cold. She could feel her legs above her knee
socks and below her skirt getting gooseflesh. Her blood,
thinned to enable her to endure the tropical heat which
was all she had ever known, felt as though it had simply
stopped and frozen solid in her veins. For a moment
it seemed to be much easier to do what this dreadful man
had said: Turn around and go back. But to where? There
could only be one answer: to that horrible children's
shelter where all the placeless, homeless, familyless
children had been temporarily herded, and where she
had left Fat Buttery and San Ignacio to come up here.
Fat Buttery might make out all right, with his joyous blue
eyes and roly-poly yellow curls and sunny disposition.
Or at least he would until the moment he thought she
had abandoned him. At which point his world, which
had collapsed once or twice before, would come to an
end again.

With San Ignacio things would be even more difficult.
For one thing they might forget to include the Saint part
of his name when they addressed him, which always
drove him wild. For another he was brown, which meant
that they might put him and Fat Buttery in different
sections because of the difference in color or even because of the difference in age. For yet another, San Ignacio sometimes lived in a world he had invented, which
he found entirely satisfactory as did everybody else as
long as they remembered that and took it into considera-
tion. If they didn't—

"I said, I would drive you to the bus station," the man
almost barked.

Alison looked up at him. She simply couldn't be put off now. Too much hung on it. "I'd like to come in and get warm first," she said. "Please. It's terribly cold out here."

"You can get warm at the bus station. I'll call the people who sent you up here, so they can meet you at the other end."

Alison continued to look up at him. She was trying desperately to think of something that would get him to move just a bit one way or the other. Then she could slip in through the door. Once she was inside, this ogre would find it far harder to evict her.

"Please!" she said. By thinking hard about Fat Buttery and San Ignacio in the dreary shelter crammed with children she had no trouble at all squeezing out several large tears.

The man looked, if possible, more exasperated. But he said, gruffly, "All right. For five minutes. Until you warm up. Then I'm taking you to the bus station."

"Thank you," Alison said.

He moved back and she stepped inside.

The house was not quite as dilapidated inside as out. But it was certainly not cozy. There was a big gloomy hall from which opened out two rooms that looked equally gloomy. Alison followed her Cousin Nicholas back, through a door, into the kitchen, which wasn't particularly cheerful either. But it was warm. The heat came from a huge old-fashioned range. Through a grating, Alison could see the red of a coal fire.

"Oh, lovely!" she said, and went up to it, spreading out her hands.

"Don't put your hands on top, you'll burn the skin off," her cousin said crossly. "I'll make some tea. That'll heat you faster than anything else."

"Thank you, Uncle Nicholas. That would be marvelous!"

"And I'm not your Uncle Nicholas, so don't call me that."

"What would you like me to call you?" Alison turned her back to the fire and raised her skirt a little so that her frozen backside could get warm.

"Since you're leaving immediately, you won't need to call me anything."

Alison didn't say anything. Her cousin handed her a cup of hot, sweet tea which tasted very good indeed and put some courage into her. She stared down at the cup as she slowly sipped it. Somehow, she had to persuade him not only to let her stay, but let her go back to the shelter and return with Fat Buttery and San Ignacio. It seemed impossible, but the holy man had always said that with God all things were possible. The people at the mission who had looked after her when her father died had always told her that she shouldn't talk to the holy man because he belonged to the wrong religion and worshipped the wrong God. But her father had never believed that, and the holy man had been a good friend of his.

"With God," Alison said aloud to cheer herself on, "all things are possible."

Her cousin turned around. "What did you say?"

"My friend, the holy man, always said that. That with God, all things are possible."

"Such as?"

"Well, I have two brothers." Alison rearranged the truth slightly. "They'll come to live here, too. You'll like them."

"Unfortunately, I won't have the pleasure of meeting them." He took her empty cup. "Come along now."

"But they're not female. You said, you really said, you didn't like females. If they were here, too, they would sort of, well, make up for the fact of me being a female. We're your *cousins*. You can't put us out. It's dark and I haven't had any sleep and I'm hungry and besides there isn't any other bus today, and if there were I couldn't go because I don't have any money." And at that point, with no planned effort at all, Alison burst into tears.

The man stood there like a furious bull who wanted to charge but, for reasons beyond his control, couldn't. Finally he said, "That's why I don't like females. They're always bursting into tears. Here!"

Alison found herself clutching a large handkerchief. "You're kind after all," she said hopefully.

"No, I'm not kind. And don't get any ideas because I lent you my handkerchief. I don't like runny noses. Now, I have a cousin in Westchester, married, with children of her own. Didn't you try her? Or the other one in Connecticut, also married. Either one of them would be perfect. I told you I'm a bachelor."

Alison gave her nose a final polish. "I don't mind. About your being a bachelor. Truly!"

"But I do. What about them? Have you investigated them?"

Alison had. The memories of the day she spent at one of those well regulated households had haunted her ever since. They made her feel as though she came from another (and inferior) planet. And while they might

eventually tame and bend Fat Buttery into their mold
(he'd broken two Spode cups and had had an unhouse-
broken accident on the oriental carpet), they'd probably
drive San Ignacio mad by trying to change him.

Also, it had been extremely hard to explain why her
brother San Ignacio was brown when she and Fat Buttery were not. And to crown everything else, San Ignacio
had wrapped himself in his raincoat, which he had been
forced to use since they had taken away his blanket, had
retreated to the corner of the elegant living room, and,
sitting cross-legged behind his raincoat, had glared at
them.

"He's disturbed," the Westchester cousins had said.

"No," Alison had explained. "He's praying."

"Well, if he's praying, why is he scowling so dread-
fully? And why is he gnashing his teeth?"

"He's probably praying that lightning will come down
and strike you."

"That doesn't sound very Christian. I thought you
were all brought up in a mission."

"Yes, but it never really took with San Ignacio. He said
he liked his own gods better."

Alison, who knew that San Ignacio was putting on the
whole show probably to turn the Westchester cousins
off. Therefore she was considerably disappointed when
instead of recoiling with horror from the heathen, they
started talking immediately about comparative religions
and tolerance and understanding. But his color still
disturbed their sense of genetics.

"But your mother was so fair," Alison's father's
third cousin twice removed said. "You're sallow—well,
olive-skinned—but so was your father. But Ignacio—

And anyway, I never heard that your parents had more children. Of course we didn't hear often."

San Ignacio bared his teeth and growled like a dog.

"You must call him *San* Ignacio. It's important," Alison said.

"But SAN Ignacio," the cousin continued, eyeing him nervously, "is definitely brown. According to Mendel's law . . . And your mother died years before that other little boy—what is it you call him?"

But it was at that moment that Fat Buttery had had his mishap. The third cousin twice removed had spent the rest of the time talking about how few bedrooms she had and how dangerous the local schools were, and promptly after tea they all went back to the mission shelter. All three were relieved. It was crowded, smelly, gloomy, totally chaotic and the food was terrible. But it was the nearest thing to what home had been and no one thought them at all strange.

The Connecticut cousins never suggested that they come up.

"Yes," Alison said now, turning the sodden handkerchief around and around in her hand. "They didn't want us."

"Well, other arrangements will have to be made. As I've said repeatedly, you can't stay here."

"There isn't a bus until tomorrow afternoon. Do I have to sleep there tonight and sit there all tomorrow? It's cold."

Nicholas MacBain glared at her, reminding Alison of San Ignacio. "Is that the truth or did you make it up?"

"It's the truth," Alison put as much outrage as she

could in her tone.

"Would you tell a lie if you thought you could further your cause?"

"Yes," Alison replied, before she had time to think, tripped by a long habit of truthfulness. Her cheeks turned pink. One rather grubby hand went up in front of her mouth.

Something that might have been the beginning of a smile started into his eyes but vanished so fast that Alison decided it must have been her imagination or wishful thinking.

"In that case, I'll check." He went out. Alison could hear him dialing from another room. Then she heard him growl something into a phone. Then he said, "Thank you," and came back into the kitchen.

"Well, you were telling the truth this time. There isn't a bus until tomorrow afternoon."

Alison hastily debated tactics. Then she gave a huge yawn. "If you can just show me where I can sleep, I'll go to bed. I'm very tired."

He was staring at her closely in the fading light. "How old are you?"

Why was that the one question that any adult could always be depended upon to ask? Alison wondered. Was it that important? "Eleven. And one month."

"You look younger. But you sound older. In fact, you don't sound like any child I've ever had the misfortune of knowing, or like any of the brats around the village here."

That was a pretty frequent remark, too. Alison's brief and unhappy experience of children brought up in the ordinary way in ordinary families had led her to believe she was very odd indeed. "I know," was all she could think to say. She gave another yawn.

She really was tired. It had been a long day, starting before dawn back in New York where the frantic woman in charge of finding relatives and homes for the mission children put her on the bus. Her last words had been, "There must be a Mrs. MacBain. You'll like it up there; it's country. And if it's a big enough house and they're willing to take in two strangers, you can come back for Peter John and St. Ignatius." (Peter John was the baptismal name of Fat Buttery.)

"They are *not* strangers. They're my brothers. I told you," Alison said sharply, one foot on the bus. She was determined to stick to her lie through thick and thin, else how would the three be adopted together? And she was quite prepared to take her foot off the bus now and go back to the mission shelter if there was any question of tampering with the two boys while she was away.

"Yes, dear. I know you did. But the letters and papers said nothing about it. And you shouldn't have told that fib to your cousins."

"If you let anything at all happen to Fat Buttery or San Ignacio, I won't go." And she took her foot off the bus step.

"Either you get in now or we go without you," the bus driver said crossly. It was a terrible hour and his eyes were pink.

Alison looked at him. "He was drinking last night, you can tell by the eyes," she informed her companion in a conversational voice. "At the mission in—"

"What did you say?"

"Who said—?"

Both the driver and the woman spoke at once. Both, for entirely different reasons, looked outraged.

"Get in," the woman said, pushing Alison's skinny form up the step.

"Not until you promise that you won't move or do anything to Fat Buttery or San Ignacio."

"All right. I promise." There was amazing strength in the slight body. Besides, she couldn't physically force her difficult charge on the bus.

"Swear on the Bible!" Alison yelled, her knees and back rigid as she braced herself against the woman's hands.

"On the Bible I give my word. It's wrong to swear. Please get in, Alison. Fat B—I mean Peter John and St. Ignatius will be here when you get back. Maybe they can go up there."

"Kids!" the driver said with loathing, watching Alison worm her way to the back of the bus. "They ain't got no respect these days."

It had been a tiring day.

"I'll go to bed now," Alison now told MacBain. "We can discuss bringing my brothers tomorrow. You'll like us. We'll keep house for you. Fat Buttery is almost housebroken and San Ignacio makes beautiful tortillas."

"Either I'm going out of my mind or I'm hallucinating," MacBain said. "Can't you understand English? You're not staying and your brothers are certainly not coming here."

Alison gave him a long look. "You're racially prejudiced. Just like the others."

"What the—what on earth are you talking about? What have I got to be prejudiced about? Or who?"

"Whom," Alison corrected. "San Ignacio. Because he's brown. That's why you think you mind about him coming here."

"His," MacBain said unthinkingly.

"His what?"

"*His* coming here. 'Coming' is an adjectival participle and takes the possessive adjective, not pronoun."

"Don't you like brown people?"

"Please go to bed. This is more conversation than I've had to endure in six months."

"It's very kind of you to invite me."

"I didn't."

"Why don't you show me which bed?"

"Just keep on going upstairs till you get to the attic."

"Do you have a bathroom?"

"There's one next door to your attic."

"I think you and I are going to be friends."

"We won't have time. You're leaving tomorrow."

2

Alison slept in a large room under the eaves. It was warmed by a huge pipe that came straight up from the kitchen range. There were dormer windows which, since it was night, were quite black when she went up. A lot of faded carpets and rag rugs were on the floor. There were a desk, a bureau, a table, two or three chairs, two chests and an old fashioned trunk around the walls and a bed and another table and some chairs in the middle. The bed, which was small but surprisingly comfortable, was covered with old quilts and an eiderdown. She had meant to think out a whole plan for getting San Ignacio and Fat Buttery up here, a plan that got around the present difficulties of no money and what appeared to be her cousin's determination to get rid of her. But the day had been more wearing than she realized. She was asleep a second after her head sank into the soft, down pillow.

When she woke up, Alison found she was on her side and staring straight through one of the low dormer windows to the end of the headland and beyond that, the sea. She was filled with wonder at its beauty. The sky still had some of its pink and gold dawn feathers, and the sea, with the eastern sun on it, was somewhere between emerald and turquoise. Alison lay there a minute, not stirring or turning. After a while, without a sound, she started to cry. She didn't know whether she was crying because the emerald sea was so beautiful or because she also felt terribly lonely without San Ignacio and Fat Buttery. Both were orphans and she had looked after them almost all their lives, first at the mission in India, until it closed for lack of funds and supplies, and then in a small village in the Andes, when that closed for the same reason.

The trouble with their missions, Alison had once overheard in a conversation between two missionaries, was that they belonged to no established church or group. Started on impulse by a midwestern church after an emotional sermon on foreign missions, the one or two mission posts established had gone gently downhill through lack of skill, languages and evangelical know-how. Those who saw this right away and were serious about their calling joined some better organized group. Others, devout but impractical, died of various tropical diseases for which they had not been inoculated. Alison's parents and those of Fat Buttery had been among

the latter. San Ignacio had simply been found in the
mission grounds in India at the age of two with his name,
St. Ignatius, printed on a piece of paper pinned to his
diaper. One or two of the more straight-laced of the
missionaries had tried to give him a less pointedly
Catholic name, but he refused to respond to anything
else, so they had abandoned the struggle. Both children
had been handed to Alison to take care of, so that, at the
age of eight, she was their mother as well as being a
part-time Sunday School teacher and an occasional
assistant at the small first aid station run by the mission.
She loved being their mother. It had filled a great gap
in her life. So she fed and emptied, cleaned, taught,
played with, comforted and loved first St. Ignatius (who
became San Ignacio when they all moved from India to
the Andes and who came to identify himself fiercely
with the South American Indian, blanket, tortillas and
all) and later Fat Buttery.

In the course of her brief years, Alison had helped out
during floods, unfriendly attacks, fever epidemics, even,
in a pinch, giving a hand at delivering one or two babies.
She had been chased through a jungle, half eaten by
mosquitos, expected to read two chapters of the Bible
every day and five on Sunday so she would get through
it in a year, taught to cook everything that was remotely
edible and a few things that were not, and how to suck
out the poison if one is bitten by a snake. By none of that
was she dismayed or frightened.

What frightened her more than anything on earth was
children of her own age whom she had met at her
cousins and at the homes of other well-wishing people.
This occurred when the mission, after yet another flood
and a final attack, finally closed and returned to the

States. The seven adults and three children were now temporarily lodged in a decaying house somewhere south of Greenwich Village in Manhattan, where they fought cockroaches, the city housing commission and their landlord.

Slowly, the adults found homes or jobs, or at least the expectation of them. But Alison, San Ignacio and Fat Buttery remained a problem. None of the ex-missionaries could afford to take them. The original church that had sent them out, its missionary impulse of yesteryear forgotten, now had a different congregation in what amounted to an entirely different neighborhood, its original members having one by one moved away. There was no help there.

The obvious thing to do was to split up the three children in the hope that, separately, they would find homes. That meant, of course, that Fat Buttery would immediately be adopted. Who could resist his Anglo Saxon charm, his three-year-old grin and his merry nature? But Fat Buttery, though only three, had a firmer grasp of reality than he had been credited with. He didn't at all mind being picked up, hugged, kissed, oohed and aahed at, cuddled and bounced as long as Alison and San Ignacio were there. When the most eager of his would-be adoptive parents took him home, alone, for an experimental week, disaster occurred.

At one end Alison and San Ignacio sat uneating and mostly unsleeping, Alison in a chair, San Ignacio wrapped in a blanket on the floor, tearless and silent. San Ignacio's warm brown face turned a sort of gray. Alison started looking like a little old woman. At the other end Fat Buttery began to howl in the car as soon as he realized the rest of his personal family was left behind. Except for rare and brief intervals, he had not stopped. The only two creatures that had meaning for him were mysteriously lost. He slapped food away, ignored the many and expensive presents that were waiting for his coming, lost his frail hold on the civilized behavior known as being housebroken, and worked himself into such hysterics that the couple, momentarily beaten, brought him back. Alison and San Ignacio rushed to the door, picked him up, hugged him between them and carried him off to their favorite warm spot in the kitchen. Ten minutes later the beet color had left his face, his blue eyes, no longer drenched, were once again joyous, and he was eating as much fudge cake as Alison and San Ignacio between them could shove into his mouth.

Two weeks later the couple were back with a compromise: they would also take Alison.

"What about San Ignacio?" Alison asked them.

"Well," they said, "perhaps later. It's a bit difficult..."

Even the desperate ex-missionaries, with eviction notices arriving daily in the mail boxes, refused to listen to that.

That was when the three were sent off to visit Alison's relatives.

Fat Buttery was an immediate success. San Ignacio could have been, but despite considerable overtures, he refused to talk or do anything but glare. But Alison, encountering for the first time non-missionary children her own age, learned the ashy taste of being an outsider. She was sent to the "den" with her cousins and their friends. After the first polite exchanges were over, they asked her where she went to school.

Alison told them one of the missionaries—whichever one happened to be least busy at the moment—taught her, and she taught San Ignacio and Fat Buttery.

They looked taken aback. "Oh. What subject?"

"The Bible, of course." Alison said, pointing out the (to her) obvious. A second later she added, "Also the local language and arithmetic."

"Weirdo," one of her cousins said. "I mean—what about social science and ecology?"

Alison wanted to ask "What's that?" But before these arrogant, sophisticated contemporaries she didn't want to display ignorance. "Oh," she said carelessly, "that came later."

She sat there looking at them in their jeans or plaid skirts and sweaters, and they looked at her, dressed by the good missionaries in what they thought suitable for meeting and spending the day with one's well-to-do relatives: a red velveteen dress, showing rather visibly the signs of having been made over from something else, a tacky white lace collar, black stockings and laced shoes. Alison was not a pretty child. Her features were nondescript, her dark brown hair lank and inclined to divide over her prominent ears, and her eyes an amber color that made her look the same color all over. When she was excited and engaged on one of her projects, the amber eyes seemed to turn into a gold blaze. Her face became not good-looking, but vivid and packed with life. She exuded energy and imagination. When she was ill-at-ease or felt frightened or inadequate, that light drained out and it was hard to imagine it had ever been there. She looked like an uninteresting mouse.

Her cousins and their school friends regarded her with diminishing interest. Further questions had elicited the facts that she had never seen television, never been to a movie, didn't know what rock music was and was totally uninterested in the subject of boy friends. On the other hand, she was not different enough from them to be exotic as, for example, San Ignacio was, and they felt frustrated that he would not communicate with them in any way.

"Why does he hold that crummy old raincoat around him like that?" her cousin asked.

"He uses it as a blanket. Mrs. Daniels thought it would be better if he didn't bring his blanket today. It's worn and rather dirty."

"Wow, too much! His security blanket for real."

Alison didn't know what a security blanket was either. But she was a fast learner and she wasn't going to give these patronizing cousins of hers any excuse for despising her by showing more ignorance. She didn't understand all that they said. But she did understand their tone.

"You don't know what you're talking about. All you do is read books. You don't know anything real.

Her older cousin flared up in defense. "It's a pity you don't read more books. You seem to be stuffed full of old-fashioned, outmoded ideas."

The younger one giggled. "Maybe she can't read."

One of the guests said, "Old ideas match old clothes." And they all went off into smothered giggles.

Alison, burning with rage, fear and humiliation, decided to go downstairs before she cried.

When she left, the others looked at one another. They felt rather ashamed.

When Alison got downstairs, Fat Buttery, in disgrace over the broken cup and the puddle on the carpet, was howling. San Ignacio, standing rigid as a poker with his raincoat properly on and buttoned, was holding the sobbing and sodden Fat Buttery by the hand. The adults looked vaguely distraught but seemed, without success, to be trying to reassure the two boys.

"Let us go," San Ignacio said to Alison in formal Spanish. "This is not an agreeable or *simpatico* place."

"Yes. Let's." She snatched her own coat and hat off the hat stand in the hall.

"I'm extremely sorry, Cousin Pamela," she addressed her cousin, "that we have to go back now. Immediately."

Cousin Pamela, guilty and relieved, was about to get the car when the four girls came downstairs.

"Are you going?" they asked, surprised.

Alison looked up at them. "Yes." She took San Ignacio's hand. "Come along," But when, after pushing them ahead of her through the front door, she started to step out herself, she looked back at her four tormentors.

"And if San Ignacio wants to wear a blanket like his friends there's no reason he shouldn't."

"What was that all about?" Cousin Pamela asked her on the way to the station.

Alison took a firm grip of San Ignacio's hand beside her and tightened her arm around Fat Buttery, who was on her lap and now thoughtfully sucking his thumb. "Just a discussion," she said airily. The nearer she got to New York the better she felt.

Now, lying on her side in the bed, looking out at the green sea, she reflected that everything, however unpleasant, had led to her coming up here to Cousin Nicholas's. She knew, in her bones, it was right for all three of them. The house was perfect. Her Cousin

Nicholas? Well, he must simply be persuaded. And with or without his permission, San Ignacio and Fat Buttery must be brought up by some means or other, however impossible it looked. And the sooner the better. She trusted Mrs. Daniels and the remaining adults in the ramshackle house in New York. But they were all soon to go away, and if a home for Alison, San Ignacio and Fat Buttery—all together—had not been found, if the city or the state had suddenly caught on to their orphaned, unschool-attending status—

But Alison drove back the chorus of negatives. Sitting up she said firmly, "With God, all things are possible."

Then she got out of bed, bathed and dressed hurriedly and went downstairs.

She had hoped and expected to be the first by an hour or so, by which time she would have fixed an eye-catching, stomach-warming breakfast. This would not only soothe the savage breast of her Cousin Nicholas, but give a splendid first demonstration of how useful she would be. She had made breakfast in far stranger places and under far more challenging conditions than a New England kitchen owned by a surly bear of a human being.

As she approached the bottom of the steps leading into the gloomy little hall, she reminded herself that nothing was impossible. She did this to counteract a tendency on the part of her knees to feel a little watery. Tiptoeing, so as not to make any unnecessary noise, she went through a sort of swing door into the kitchen. Then she stopped, dismayed. The big table in the middle of the kitchen had a place on it laid for one with a cup, a bowl, a pitcher and a spoon. Standing, looking out the window with his back to her, was MacBain.

Then he turned around, and Alison saw he was holding a steaming cup.

"Good morning," Alison said as brightly as she could over her disappointment. "I was going to fix breakfast for you."

MacBain ignored the greeting. "I've eaten. I prefer to cook for myself. There's oatmeal and coffee on the stove, bread, milk and sugar on the table. Take what you want."

Alison had had many things for breakfast, including breadfruit, rice, raw fish and nothing at all, but never oatmeal.

She helped herself to a sticky spoonful, poured a little coffee in her cup and then filled the rest of the cup with milk. Nervously she took a small bite of the oatmeal and chewed and chewed and chewed. MacBain was watching her.

"Haven't you eaten oatmeal before?"

"No."

"Well, it's easier with sugar and milk."

"Oh." She helped herself to both. "Yes. You're right. It is," she said brightly. Eating very slowly, she looked around the kitchen, hoping to find something undone, some dirt uncleaned, some corner undusted, an unwashed plate or unmended clothes. If there were no visible way in which she could show herself to be needed—but in her life there had always been too much to do. Nothing in her preparation or training allowed for not having to do anything. The oatmeal, which she found unpleasant, seemed to be lying like a lump of iron in the general region of her chest. But she was intensely aware that her cousin was looking at her.

"When you're finished," he spoke up, "I'll get the car out."

Panic gripped her. "But the bus doesn't go until this afternoon. You called and found out."

"There's another bus from the next town east leaving for New York in about two hours. I'll put you on that."

Desperation required desperate measures. "I haven't finished my breakfast."

"We have plenty of time. It's only about twenty-five miles. Have all you want."

✗   The mere thought of eating any more of that gluey substance made the undissolved lump in her chest quiver. The only thing in Alison's life that had ever given her any trouble was a tendency towards a queasy stomach when she was nervous.

"Thank you," she said politely. "It's delicious."

"Then you have a very finicky way of eating something you describe as delicious."

"One shouldn't gobble." Alison said virtuously. She picked up her plate, carried it over to the range, took two large spoonfuls of the oatmeal and returned to her place. It seemed to her that the contents of her bowl looked lumpier than before. Her chest—or was it her stomach?—quivered again. Bravely she poured a lot of sugar and a large dollop of milk on top. Then she closed her eyes. It was plain to her that she needed all the help she could get. And she had forgotten grace when she sat down. Perhaps that was what was wrong with the oatmeal.

"Bless, O Lord, this food for our use and us to Thy service," she said loudly, and picked up her spoon.

The first two mouthfuls went down without too much

trouble. She was rather hesitant about following them with a third until they settled. A quick glance showed she was being watched. The quivering in her chest increased. She ran her spoon slowly around in the milk. If she took a lot of milk in each spoonful, and a very little oatmeal, she just might—

"You might as well stop torturing yourself with that stuff. Your delaying tactics are not getting you—"

But at that moment there was a loud rapping on the front door.

"Who the—" MacBain started, scowling.

Another rat-tat.

Grateful for the diversion, Alison sprang towards the door. "I'll see who it is," she called, and heard an angry shout, which she ignored.

Plunging through the swing door she ran through the dark hall towards the front door and flung it open. On the doorstep was a man in an overcoat, rimless glasses and a disagreeable expression.

He was plainly not expecting to see her. He had a piece of paper in his hand and was about to speak, but stopped. "Who are you?"

"I'm—" Alison started, but MacBain spoke behind her. "What do you want, Sanders?"

"You've had fair warning, not once but three times. Now I have here a letter from the bank, ordering you to vacate. You know very well this house belongs to the bank and was only rented to you on a month-to-month basis—"

"Only because the bank wanted to sell it. But in the run-down state this house was in nobody would buy it, so you were glad enough to rent it to me. And I have not only paid the rent regularly, I recently put in electricity and running water—"

A smug look settled over Mr. Sanders' prim features. "Exactly. That's just the point. Where did you get the money to do anything so expensive? In view of the fact that you do no visible work, we find your sudden — er —wealth highly suspicious."

MacBain unexpectedly grinned. "So that's what's bothering you! I might have known it! That's precisely why I do my banking in the next town, in somebody else's bank, so you can't snoop into my account to see where my—er—income comes from. And it's nearly killing you with jealousy and curiosity!"

Mr. Sanders' mouth drew up like a purse. "How dare you! You're just trying to prevent me from doing my duty. You're to vacate no later than—"

But Alison, who had been listening to this conversation with rising alarm, saw her dream disappearing. "You can't do that!" she wailed.

MacBain tried to push her back. "Pay no attention to her," he said.

But Mr. Sanders was fixing her with an astonished look. "Why not, young lady?"

Two things happened. The first was that Alison had a heaven-sent (she hoped) inspiration. She took a deep breath. "Because I'm his long lost daughter come to live with him."

The second was, she threw up.

3

A few minutes later Alison was lying on an old-fashioned wooden settle in the kitchen, looking pale and feeling miserable but listening with great interest to the two men squabble.

"I suppose you've been bullying her the way you bully everybody else," the man named Sanders said. "Here your own daughter—"

"I keep telling you," MacBain bit out each word. "She is not my daughter." He was at the sink furiously washing his hands after disposing of the remains of Alison's accident. "She simply turned up yesterday claiming some sort of remote relationship."

Alison gave a low moan and held her stomach. Both men turned. "Father," she breathed. "Can't you take away the pain?"

Even MacBain's beard seemed to bristle. "I am not your father. Don't you dare try that! And if you'd refrained from shoveling in that oatmeal—"

"Irresponsible as always!" Sanders' voice rose. "Irresponsible when you stole that money, irresponsible when you refused to admit you'd done it or to restore it, and now irresponsible when you won't acknowledge or, I suppose, even help this unfortunate child and her probably equally unfortunate mother!"

"I am not—" MacBain started furiously.

"Mother's dead," Alison said, and gave away to a general desire to cry, which was always very easy right after she threw up. "She died far away crying for my father." Which was entirely true and exactly what the good missionaries had told her long after the event. Her mother had succumbed to some tropical infection while her husband was too far away baptising new converts—to be reached.

Sanders looked at MacBain with the prissy scorn of a man who had never had any children and thus had been able to retain sentimental views about their innocence and lack of guile.

"I should have guessed. It's exactly like everything else in your heedless, selfish life from the time you embezzled money from my bank—"

"I did not embezzle your blankety blank money," MacBain roared, slamming his hand on the table and knocking the half-filled bowl of oatmeal off onto the floor. "And since you obviously couldn't prove that I did—"

"And *you* couldn't prove that silly, made-up story of being in Boston all that day—"

"—and not only leaving me," Alison said, suddenly remembering San Ignacio and Fat Buttery, "but my two brothers—half-brothers," she amended, remembering her cousin's bafflement about San Ignacio's brownness.

"Three helpless orphans," the banker said, "three sweet innocent children, abandoned! It passes belief!"

"Innocent my foot!" MacBain shouted. "That lying urchin over there is making the whole thing up. I don't know how she got here or who sent her, but she's going back on the—" he glanced at the old-fashioned clock on the kitchen wall and bent an angry glare on Alison. "Well, you've succeeded in foiling me in getting you on the morning bus. But I can assure you you'll be on the afternoon bus from the village."

"And where will these wretched children go without a home, may I ask?" Sanders inquired, in the tone he used for his frequent speeches before the Town Assembly.

"I neither know nor care," MacBain said. "I need solitude and peace in which to write. If I'd wanted children I would have married and had them."

"We must assume you are deceiving us about this as you have about everything else. And furthermore, may I say your writing seems to have been singularly unsuccessful. Not one published story, let alone a book."

Above the neatly trimmed beard MacBain's cheeks went red. "I've told you. I prefer to write under a pen name."

"*If* that is true, which I doubt, that means your work is not fit for the eyes of these sweet, innocent—"

"If you call that truthless child over there sweet and innocent one more time—"

Alison, who was feeling much better, decided she had been quiet long enough. "Father, you promised," she said pleadingly. In the back of her mind and conscience all the upright, truth-telling principles in which she had been drilled clamored protestingly. But, far stronger were not only the urgent needs of San Ignacio and Fat Buttery, but a growing enjoyment in her dramatic role. "Father," she repeated in a voice that would have done justice to a slave at the feet of Nero, and clasping her hands. "You promised."

One thing must be said of Mr. Sanders: Alison could not have asked for an audience more suited to her needs.

He cleared his throat, got out his large handkerchief and blew.

"I promised you nothing except to put you on the first possible bus," MacBain roared. "You deceitful girl! You're just like every other woman!"

Sanders emerged from his handkerchief. "I'll have no ugly aspersions on the fairer sex. Perhaps a good woman—"

"There's no such thing," MacBain interrupted rudely. I had six older sisters, so I should know."

"As I was saying, a good woman might have saved you from yourself. And furthermore," he raised his voice as MacBain was obviously about to interrupt again. "I'll tell you this. If indeed you give a decent home to this unfortunate girl and her brothers, I think I can assure you that the bank will take a different view of your continued and unwanted residence on its property—"

"The *bank* isn't trying to get rid of me. *You* are,"

MacBain said, and added drily, "And I think I know why."

"I *am* the bank," Mr. Sanders said simply. He put the eviction notice that he had been holding back in his pocket and puffed his lips out a little. "I think, I can almost guarantee, that the board of directors—of which I am, of course, chairman—might even be induced to accede to your frequent demand to buy the property. Subject, naturally, to certain agreements," he added quickly, as though he had forgotten something.

"That's extortion and blackmail," MacBain shouted.

"And FURTHERMORE," Sanders went on, ignoring him, "my wife and one or two other good ladies of the community will be here to see that these children of yours are properly fed and clothed. Abandoning your family! We knew something like that would turn up. Disgraceful! We may be an isolated community, old-fashioned, off the mainstream, but we know what is right and where our duty lies." He buttoned his coat and put on his hat. "I will give you a good day." And he stumped out of the kitchen.

"Pompous old bullfrog," MacBain said as soon as the banker was through the swing door. "And as for you," he said, turning towards Alison.

But Alison was lying down again, clasping her stomach. She said weakly, "I think I may throw up again."

Several hours later she was still on the settle, by now with a pillow under her head and a blanket over her, both articles ungraciously supplied by MacBain when she said a) her head hurt and her neck was stiff and b) she was cold.

"Though it would do far more good if you got up and

took a brisk walk," he said as he handed her the blanket and pillow.

Alison, who had become extremely bored with doing nothing but lying there, silently agreed. But she knew that the moment she showed the faintest sign of returning health—such as getting up—MacBain would have her at the bus station before she could give one little moan or clutch her tummy.

"However," he went on, looking down at her, "I wouldn't for the world have you anything but rested and well for your journey."

Alison glanced at him from under lowered eyelids, trying to find one sign of warmth or kindness in that face. Then, still covertly watching, she gave a small sigh. "I shall have to travel all night," she said in a sad voice.

"Oh, you'll be able to sleep on the bus."

"What about Mr. Sanders and your being evicted? He said if he didn't find Fat Buttery and San Ignacio and me here the bank would take your house away."

MacBain, still standing over her, said, "Don't you worry your little head about that. Neither he nor the bank is going to move me one foot."

"If they bring a policeman, how could you stop them?"

"There's only one policeman, and I'm bigger than he is."

Alison at that moment wished with all her heart that she had her unpleasant cousin on her side. He might be gruff, inhospitable and off-putting—although there were moments when Alison could almost believe she glimpsed somebody different, and nicer, behind the bear-like facade. But whether she was right or not about that, there was absolutely no question that MacBain was a fighter. And not since her father had died had Alison known a real fighter. Mrs. Daniels was kind and the other missionaries meant well. But Alison, like her father, had never found them able to provide any real obstacle when she made up her mind to do something. However, to take on, single-handed, laws and state bureaus was something else. She said rather desperately, "We'll be split up and sent to an orphanage."

"What about that mission of yours? Don't they have a headquarters or home for the children of your late and lamented missionaries?"

"No. Mrs. Daniels says all the money went after the first enthusiasm, and now there isn't any. And anyway, the people are all moved away now, and finding homes takes time and they don't have any, or at least, they don't have any money to wait while somebody can be found to adopt all three of us."

MacBain had been walking restlessly around, but he came over to the settle and loomed over her again. Looking up at him, Alison's heart, not easily daunted, felt a qualm.

"I suppose," he said, "you think your sad plight and that of your brothers—if they are your brothers, which I doubt—should move my stony heart. Like Scrooge, I should stop saying 'Bah Humbug!' and take you all in, revealing, under this exterior, a heart of gold."

"Yes," Alison said, sitting up. "I do."

"Well, my inside is just as tough as my outside. If I had any interest to spare—which I don't—from what I was doing, I might think about your plight and decide it was up to one of our family-minded cousins to deal with it. But I have interest only in what I am doing—writing. And your being here would get in the way of that. I can't write if anybody's in the house."

"That man said you couldn't write anyhow. That you've never had anything published."

Apparently that was a tender nerve. The cheeks above the beard got red again. "That's not true."

"Then why do you blush when anybody says it?"

"Because—never mind. It's none of your business. And I'll have you know that's *my* settle you're lying on under *my* blanket in *my* house. It would be well if you kept a civil tongue in your head."

"Mrs. Daniels, who taught me composition, said I write very well. Perhaps I could help you?"

"Heaven forfend!"

"What does that mean?"

"It means no."

Alison sat back again. "It seems to me," she said after a moment, "you're in no position to turn down help. You need us."

"It's time to leave for the bus."

"I don't feel well."

"If you feel well enough to argue my arm off, you feel well enough to take the bus."

"You'll get put out of your house. And anyway—" she sat up, suddenly remembering a really interesting part of the conversation that in her preoccupation with her own needs she had forgotten. "He said you stole money from the bank. That's wicked. Did you?" And then she really was scared. MacBain's expression had not been exactly warm before. Now it was as though cold steel rippled down her backbone. "I'm s-sorry," she said with truth.

"Don't say that now or at any other time again," he said. "Not that you will be here to do so. Now get up. We're going to the bus."

"I'm sorry. Truly I am, Cousin Nicholas. Please don't

be angry. Only why does he accuse you of doing that?"

"I don't think I owe you any explanation," he said. "Now get off the settle."

MacBain stared down at Alison and she stared back up at him. The situation had now become crucial. Rather desperately, Alison silently reminded God that with Him all things were possible.

"If you don't get up," MacBain said. "I'll carry you." And he started to lean down. Alison was quick and small and agile. She slid past his outstretched hands, landed on the floor beside the settle, and then, as MacBain, with an exclamation, lunged after her, sped through the swing door.

She was afraid if she wrestled with the front door lock he would catch up with her. So she flew up the stairs, then up into her attic and shut and locked the door. In only a second or two MacBain on the other side hammered on the wood panel. "If you don't unlock this door I'll go and get the key!"

At her wits' end, she stared around and up—and saw a skylight. The ceiling was low, so by pushing a chair underneath and standing on tiptoe, she had no trouble opening the lock and raising the glass window a little— but only a little. The hammering stopped.

"All right. I'll be back immediately." And there were footsteps receding down the attic steps.

Fear lent Alison ingenuity. Scrambling down, she placed a low stool on the chair and climbed on top of that. This way she was able to get the top half of her body onto the roof. Then she wiggled the rest of the way up. Then she lowered the skylight knowing, however, that the chair and footstool beneath would give her away. Well, it couldn't be helped. If she could just keep him away until after the bus left, then she'd have a few more hours to work with. She summoned mental images of San Ignacio and Fat Buttery. They must not go to some dreadful place where no one would love or understand them. Or where she wouldn't be able to take care of them herself.

On one side of her the roof rose steeply. On the other lay the thin gutter on which she was edging and below the grass, the cliff edge and the sea.

It was then Alison discovered that she had no head for heights. She took in one glimpse of the sea, this time purple, with the afternoon sun on it, and the green shore-line with the spruce and pine. Then everything started to go up and down like huge waves. Alison closed her eyes. *I will fall and die and they will send San Ignacio and Fat Buttery away.* It followed therefore she could not die. Cautiously she opened her eyes and stared straight in front of her. Then she glanced down, then closed her eyes again. Obviously, she must not look down. She was extremely frightened. Wildly, she hunted around for a quotation that would assist her at a time like this.

"Be strong and of a good courage," she affirmed in what she intended to be a bold, strong voice but that came out in a high squeak. At that moment she heard the skylight open. MacBain's head and shoulders appeared.

"Oh, so there you are! Haven't you any better sense than to get onto a roof? Come back!"

"Not until you promise we can live here."

"I told you. I will not be blackmailed."

Alison kept her eyes closed. "Then I am not coming in."

"Then I'll have to come and get you."

MacBain swung one leg over the skylight, chipping some of the rotten wood of the window frame. Alison

turned her face to the roof and started sliding her feet along the gutter away from him.

MacBain swung the other leg out and lowered himself onto the gutter. "It's silly for you to do that. You know I'm going to catch you, and furthermore it's dangerous." He took a long step along the gutter. There was a creak and a crack. A big piece of the gutter broke, hung for a moment and then fell with a crash. Alison gave a cry and lunged for the chimney stack and got one hand around the edge. Then she got her other arm around it and pulled herself up to a sitting position on the rooftop with her arm around the chimney stack for safety. She felt much better and looked across to Mac-Bain. He had clutched the skylight window ledge and was hanging to that with the fingertips of both hands, uttering words that Alison had been taught were wicked.

"You shouldn't swear," she said. "Toads will jump out of your mouth."

"It will be snakes and scorpions if you don't come back inside this minute." He started to wiggle up towards the skylight. A slate fell off, followed by two more.

"Perhaps you haven't kept the roof in very good repair," Alison said in a kindly voice.

MacBain groaned. "I don't know what I've done to deserve you. I've managed to keep Sanders and his gaggle of old women off my neck for the past ten years, but now, when at last I have some money to buy the house and put it in decent condition and assure my peace and quiet and solitude and independence, some malignant fate has dumped you on me." He started to draw himself up some more. Another slate fell.

"Perhaps," Alison said, in the tone of one willing to consider all sides of a question, "God doesn't wish you to have peace and quiet. Perhaps he wants you to take care of us."

"I cannot be having this conversation. This cannot be happening. I cannot be hanging on my own roof while some undersized demon is tormenting me. This is a nightmare. In a minute I'll wake up." He closed his eyes.

"I'm not undersized. And it's very rude of you to comment if I am. I am extremely sensitive about my size — just as you are about the writing you say you do and you don't."

"I keep telling you, I DO."

Two more slates slid down and crashed.

"On the other hand," Alison said. "Perhaps He wants us to take care of you. Yes, I expect that's it."

"NO! I will not have you take care of me. I won't have you in the house at all. In fact—"

At that, there was a snap, and a piece of the rotten wood of the windowsill broke off in MacBain's hand. He gave a great yell, then slid off the roof onto the ground.

"Are you hurt?" Alison called.

MacBain sat up on the grass and held his head for a while.

"Are you hurt?" Alison repeated.

MacBain raised his head and glowered at her. "If this were just a few hundred years ago, I could have you burned for a witch."

"It's not my fault your house is in poor repair. 'Except the Lord build the house'—"

"Don't quote at me!" yelled her infuriated cousin. "I can't stand any more." He tried to get up and then sat down again holding his ankle. "Oh, no!"

"What's the matter?"

"My ankle's broken."

There was the noise of a car. In a few seconds it appeared where the road curved towards the house and then stopped. Mr. Sanders got out, followed by a brown eight-year-old boy wearing an Indian band around his long black hair, a blanket over his coat and trousers, and holding by the hand a square bundle with legs at one end and a face topped by bubbling yellow curls on the other.

"San Ignacio, Fat Buttery!" Alison yelled, waving frantically with one hand. "Here I am!"

Fat Buttery broke loose and hurled himself towards the house. "Alithon, Alithon!" he cried. As he ran he divested himself of one garment after another until by the time he reached MacBain he was naked.

"Why does he take his clothes off?" Mr. Sanders asked in a shocked voice, following at a more sedate pace with San Ignacio and picking up the discarded garments as he came.

"He prefers to be naked," San Ignacio explained. "What are you doing up there, Alison? It is not appropriate for you, a female, to be on a roof. As the oldest male and therefore the head of the family, I must insist you get down."

"I'm a little puzzled by your exact relationship—" Mr. Sanders said tentatively.

"My mother, who was an Inca princess, married Alison's father as his second wife," San Ignacio said without a pause.

"But Alison's *father*—she told me herself—is Nicholas MacBain, who lives in this house and who seems to be sitting on the grass, I cannot imagine why."

San Ignacio looked at Mr. Sanders for a long minute. Then he walked over to MacBain, who was sitting muttering to himself, with Fat Buttery trying to climb on his back.

"*Padre*, Father, I salute you. It is I, your son, San Ignacio. We will now be together."

"I know this is a nightmare," MacBain said, trying to unclasp Fat Buttery's stranglehold. "If I can just concentrate I'll wake up and it will all be over."

"I found these young people at the bus station," Mr. Sanders said sternly, "waiting for someone to convey them to their last remaining hope for a home, two helpless, innocent—"

"I am *not* helpless," San Ignacio said indignantly. "Juan Pedro and I were going to walk. It is only because you said we must ride with you that we decided to do you a favor."

"It brings tears to a man's eyes," Mr. Sanders went on, taking off his spectacles and wiping them with a handkerchief and roughing out the talk he was planning for the community drive dinner the following week. "To think that there should be any question about housing these innocent—"

With a yell MacBain got to his feet. "Go away. Get off my property. If you don't go—"

"It is the bank's property," Mr. Sanders said with great dignity, backing towards his car. "And I warn you, if any harm comes to these innocent young creatures—"

"They're about as innocent as a squad of termites. If you don't go—" And, to everyone's amazement, propelled by rage, MacBain started to hop on one foot towards the banker. Mr. Sanders retreated immediately to his car. "Understand," he said with the door open, "if these innocent—"

The stick of wood slammed against the door just as he shut it. He rolled down the window. "There is never the slightest need for intemperate behavior. What have you done to your foot?"

"Thanks to your meddling, this gremlin sitting on MY roof maneuvered me into a position where I could do nothing but fall off and break my ankle."

A thin smile touched the banker's mouth. "Well, well, you seem to have met your match, MacBain. Remember now, any attempt to abandon your children—whichever ones are indeed your children—and the bank will send back the eviction notice."

"You can send the militia for all I care. No one is evicting me. And furthermore, these . . . these children"—he spoke the word through clenched teeth—"will be packed onto the first available moving vehicle and sent back to New York where the state can take care of them if no one else will."

Mr. Sanders looked even happier. "Not if you wish to stay in the bank's house, and certainly not if you wish to make it your own. Ta-ta." And he started to drive off. Then a few feet later he stopped and stuck his head out the window. "I'll send the doctor along for your foot. Good night, children!"

MacBain, who had taken an overambitious hop towards another stick, overbalanced and sat down abruptly. He closed his eyes and held his ankle.

"Does your ankle hurt?" Alison called from the roof.

"No, Of course not. I just like sitting here holding it."

Something touched him on the shoulder. He opened his eyes and looked up into a dark face with night-brown eyes.

"Would you like me to help you get up?" San Ignacio asked. "I am very strong."

MacBain opened his mouth to say something withering. To his own vast surprise what came out was a rather meek, "Thank you."

4

After his first "thank you" to San Ignacio, MacBain immediately regretted his politeness, seeing it as the thin edge of the wedge.

"And don't imagine that simply because I have accepted some slight assistance from you in getting into the house that I am going to permit my home to be taken over by that . . . that . . . she-demon who wished herself on me yesterday. She's brought me nothing but trouble." Gingerly MacBain lowered himself into an armchair that Alison and San Ignacio between them had lugged into the kitchen from the gloomy and depressing living room. "Ouch!" he yelled as his foot accidentally landed on the floor owing to San Ignacio's removing his support. "I thought you were supposed to be helping me!"

"I will not help you at all if you speak that way about Alison, who is our Earth Mother."

"Your what?"

"Our Earth Mother."

MacBain momentarily forgot his anger. "Where did he get that?" he asked Alison.

"From *The Golden Bough*, I expect."

"What was he doing reading *The Golden Bough?*"

Alison spread a large rug over MacBain's lap. MacBain winced as she dragged it over his foot. "Careful!"

"You're a big baby, did you know that? You make more fuss and noise than either San Ignacio or Fat Buttery put together did when we were running from the head-hunters. And San Ignacio had a broken arm and Fat Buttery a big cut on his head." As MacBain opened his mouth to protest this criticism, Alison hurried on. "San Ignacio read *The Golden Bough* because it was one of the five books that I inherited from my father. They were the Bible, *The Golden Bough*, the *Illiad* and the *Odyssey* (they were in one book), the *Bhagavad-Gita* and *The Wayward Gosling*."

As she noticed MacBain's stunned expression, she said in a kindly voice, *"The Wayward Gosling* is by Betsy Bounce. She's written lots of books, but that one's my favorite. I liked it best, next to the Bible, of course. San Ignacio liked it, too, though after his eighth birthday he thought it would be better to say he liked *The Golden Bough* because he is a boy and therefore the head of the family. He read it three times before the other missionaries knew he had it and took it away with the other books, except for the Bible and *The Wayward Gosling*. That's where he got the idea of me as Earth Mother, in *The Golden Bough*, I mean."

Alison paused, in case MacBain wanted to make some such comment as "how appropriate" or "It suits you." Since he didn't she said, carelessly, "I thought it was rather nice. Fat Buttery likes it, too."

But there was a very strange expression on MacBain's face, and he didn't say anything for a while.

"Well, anyway, I like being an Earth Mother."

MacBain came out of his trance. "You're too skinny for Earth Motherhood."

"I think it's mean of you to say that when you know how I feel about it." Alison got up and started to walk out of the kitchen.

"Where do you think you're going?"

"Since you insist on making rude and personal remarks, I see no reason why I should stay here and be insulted."

"Insulted! Just what would you call coming here uninvited—all three of you—taking over my home, putting me in a false position with that old woman in trousers, Sanders, making me fall off the roof and break my foot—"

"You did that by chasing me. It's entirely your own fault."

"—interrupting my work—"

"What work? If you're going to be rude to me, why should I believe that you do any writing? Show me a book or a story you've published. I can easily see how Mr. Sanders would find it most suspicious that you now have enough money to buy the house."

Alison continued on towards the door.

"All right, all right! I apologize. Now come back here and tell me who San Ignacio and Fat Buttery are, and why you're trying to palm them off as your brothers. No," he said, correctly interpreting the look on her face, "don't try and tell me they are your half-brothers because I wouldn't believe you. If we are going to share this house—temporarily—I should know who and what my guests are."

Alison slowly came back. "You mean you're getting reconciled to us?"

"I mean nothing of the kind."

"Then why should I tell you anything about them?"

"Because if you don't, I shall expose them, chapter and verse, to Sanders and all the good ladies he is undoubtedly going to send. And in case you're wondering how, I can prove you're no relation to them through our cousins, who have made occasional and faint efforts to keep up with your erratic parents and know perfectly well you're an only child."

"That would be the most horrible thing you could do, splitting us up like that. I think you're a wicked, cruel man even to—to think about it."

"I didn't say I would," MacBain said hastily, as tears came into Alison's eyes. "I just said I could. So why don't you tell me who they are?"

Alison came back into the middle of the kitchen and stood with her back to the range.

"Sit down," MacBain said in what, for him, was a kind voice, which meant that it was a soft growl instead of a hard one.

"No, thank you. I prefer to stand."

"Suit yourself."

After a minute Alison took a deep breath. "Our mission

was in North India. I was only about three or four myself, so I don't remember this, *actually*. But this baby was found on the chapel step wrapped up in a white diaper with the name St. Ignatius on it. Everybody knew it was left by accident by someone who thought it was the Catholic mission, which was ten miles away. And Father thought we ought to take him there. But the other missionaries thought that God had sent him to us and He wanted us to make him into a Protestant instead of a Catholic. So they named him Elmer, after the head of the mission. But whenever they called him that he just cried and wouldn't do whatever they wanted him to do."

"I don't blame him."

"No. Neither do I. So when the mission closed we took him to South America with us."

"So he's really a Hindu Indian, not a South American Indian."

"That's right. But when he wraps himself in a blanket and wears a headband, it's hard for people to realize that, even when I tell them he practices Yoga."

"How on earth did he learn Yoga in a Protestant mission?"

Alison sighed. "Father taught him. And me, too. It caused great difficulty."

"I can see where it would. Your father was an unusual missionary."

"My father was unusual in *every* way," Alison said stoutly. After a minute she added. "I miss him a lot."

MacBain grunted. "Now what about that nudist Fat Buttery, or whatever his real name is?"

"His real name is Peter John Calvin. His parents went out into the jungle and never came back. I always called him Fat Buttery because he looked so fat and buttery. San Ignacio calls him Juan Pedro because it sounds better than Pedro Juan. Mrs. Daniels calls him Peter John and some of the others at the mission called him Peter. You can see why I found it easier to call him Fat Buttery."

"That is the craziest outfit I ever heard of in all my life."

"Yes. That's what everybody said. But I liked it a lot."

"Why?"

"Well—I could do lots of things I was good at, like bandaging people and helping in the clinic and nursing some of the babies and occasionally I was allowed to do the cooking . . . " Her voice trailed off. "It's hard to explain."

"In contrast to what?"

"Well, when I visited our cousins, the Websters, the girls there asked me things I didn't know about, like what was my favorite show on television, or did I have a boyfriend or what rock group did I like."

MacBain shifted his foot and winced. "And you don't know anything about those?"

Alison shook her head.

"Ever seen a television show?"

"No."

"Or gone to a movie?"

"No. We had lantern slides of missionary trips. But I suppose that isn't the same."

"Ummm."

There was a short, rather companionable silence. Then the kitchen door burst open and a procession, consisting of San Ignacio, Fat Buttery (naked) and a tall man with a black bag, came in.

"Fat Buttery, put on your clothes," Alison said.

"Don't want to."

"Why does he have this passion for taking his clothes off?" MacBain asked.

"Well, you see, for a long time, it was easier just to let him go naked. The trouble is, he's never wanted to put on clothes since."

The tall man with the bag spoke up. "That's not going to please the good ladies of the village, who are even now getting up a committee to call on you and straighten things out. By the way, I'm Dr. Sharp."

"How do you do," Alison said politely. "What do you mean, straighten things out?"

"According to our local bush telegraph—that is, our housekeeper—my wife and I learned that the ladies have decided that it is improper for a bachelor of uncertain habits and suspicious income to have charge of three children, one of whom is a female. They're planning to divide you up. What's the matter?"

There was wail from Alison, San Ignacio and Fat Buttery.

"We must leave at once," San Ignacio. "Our bags are still packed."

The doctor was staring at them in concern. "Leave? For where? With whom?"

"It doesn't matter," San Ignacio said. "We are a family. We will not be divided. Alison! Come at once." He made a formal bow to the two men. "*Adios.*"

"Now just a minute," MacBain said.

Alison, almost at the door, turned. "I expect you're very glad, Cousin Nicholas. I'm sorry. I thought the three of us could have made you into a very acceptable father."

"I'm not your father and haven't the slightest desire to become so—acceptable or otherwise. But if you disappear I'll be blamed. I can buck Sanders and our local

police force, but not a bevy of ladies bent on good.
It'll be goodbye to any hope I may have of buying this
house."

"Don't you ever think of anything else?" Alison asked.
"I think that's selfish."

"Oh, you do!" MacBain sat up. "I'd like to know what
else you've been thinking about if it isn't a house for you
and the others. At least this is my house. I'm not trying to
take away somebody else's home—" At that point Mac-
Bain let out a yell. "What do you think you're doing?"
he asked the doctor, who had drawn up a chair and was
holding his foot.

"I'm trying to find out if you've broken a bone or
merely pulled a ligament. But with you thrashing about
and bellowing it's not easy. You're going to have to come
to the hospital for an X-ray."

"And leave my house to those three? I will not!"

"Well, if you think a broken, unset bone is going to
improve your circumstances, then you can never have
had one."

There was an uneasy pause.

"You need not be afraid," San Ignacio said haughtily.
"We will not be here when you return. Come, Alison.
Come, Juan Pedro."

"If they find those children gone," the doctor said,
"your scalp will be hung from the town hall, and you'll
find yourself out of this house before sundown."

There was another weighty silence.

The doctor said, "I think you've broken a bone. You'll
have to come to the hospital so that I can put your foot
in a cast." He got up and closed his bag. "I'll take you."

"Goodbye, Cousin Nicholas," Alison said from the
door.

Fat Buttery started to cry in his own particular fashion,

which meant opening his mouth wide, turning red in the face and making a loud noise. He kept right on doing this while Alison and San Ignacio pulled his sweater over one end and tugged on his trousers over the other.

"We might consider a cease-fire, a temporary truce for —er—mutual protection," MacBain said.

Fat Buttery, who understood far more than he found it convenient to admit most of the time, stopped howling and stared at MacBain. Alison and San Ignacio also paused.

"What do you mean?" San Ignacio asked.

"If you stayed here, temporarily, and I emphasize *temporarily*, we might get this whole thing resolved. You could find a home—all three of you—" he added hastily, "and I could buy the house."

"You're not thinking of anything but yourself," Alison said severely. "I've given up trusting you."

"Why don't you climb off your high horse? And anyway, who gave you the right to criticize me? As I should have said before, if I haven't already, you have a lot of nerve."

To everyone's surprise, San Ignacio took up for him. "That is right, Alison. You must not speak to him that way."

"Why not?"

"Because he is a man," San Ignacio explained with beautiful simplicity. "It is not fitting."

"Tut," Dr. Sharp said. "You're going to run into trouble with views like that."

MacBain gave a shout of joy. "San Ignacio, you may come and live with me whenever you want."

"And leave Alison and Juan Pedro? Of course not. It is an insult to suggest it. We all stay, or nobody stays."

Fat Buttery, who had been quietly getting out of his

clothes, ran across to MacBain. "Stay," he said, climbing on his lap. "I go hospital with you."

"Not naked you don't."

"Not at all you don't," Dr. Sharp said. "MacBain, do you have such a thing as a cane? I can prop you up on one side, but you need something on the other."

After MacBain and the doctor had gone, Alison and the others stood around. Absent-mindedly Alison and San Ignacio put Fat Buttery back into his trousers.

San Ignacio said, "Why are we not leaving before these women arrive and try to separate us?"

Alison said, as she pulled Fat Buttery's shirt over his head, "We must remember at all times that with God all things are possible. Whenever I forget that everything goes wrong. Let us have a meditation for guidance the way Father used to. I must get my egg-timer."

After Alison had brought her egg-timer downstairs and had set it for fifteen minutes, she and San Ignacio assumed the Lotus position, which is not at all difficult for skinny, agile people who are used to it, but which was entirely beyond Fat Buttery. Most of the meditation time he spent standing on his head, which he found easy. In between bouts of standing on his head he chugged slowly around the room, singing quietly to himself.

At the end of about ten minutes San Ignacio suddenly stiffened and said, "Aieee!"

"Sh!" Alison admonished.

"But—"

"Quiet. Later."

When the egg-timer pinged, Alison opened her eyes and said, "What?"

"I forgot to give you a letter. Mrs. Daniels gave it to me for you."

Running over to his bag, which was still standing in the corner, San Ignacio rummaged around for a while and then brought Alison a long envelope. "I'm sorry," he said.

Alison, tearing the envelope open, said reproachfully, "It could have been *important.*" She pulled out another envelope and a sheet of paper. Unfolding the paper she read aloud,

> Dear Alison:
>
> I am sorry I have been so muddled about every-thing. The City Marshal is sitting here with the eviction notice and it is unnerving me. Mrs. Spencer has gone to her retirement home, Miss Price has left for the Congo and I have finally accepted the unwelcome fact that I shall have to live with my daughter, who is coming shortly to pick me up in one of her several large, vulgar cars. She says she must, in Christian charity, insist that I will live with her. This means she doesn't really want me but feels it her DUTY—such a dreary thing—and will probably remind me of it every day. Dear me! How uncharitable I am—and to my own daughter! But there's nothing else I can do, so I must accept it. And besides, I shall be with my four grandchildren, which makes up for everything.
>
> I enclose a letter to your guardian, Nicholas Mac-Bain. I call him that because when the Child Welfare official arrived, that's what I told him. That you'd all been adopted by your cousin. Certainly the city would split you up, and we mustn't allow that. Alison, dear, I have a dreadful feeling that your other cousin, Mrs. Webster, is having an attack of conscience and will be driving up to see you with a proposition. Be on your guard! She reminds me of

my daughter. I will send you my address as soon
as I am settled.

Be strong and of a good courage. (Joshua, 1.9)
Priscilla Daniels

P. S. Why is it that I found headhunters and even
cannibals easier to deal with than city officials?
Oh dear—I'm rambling again!

"I can easily see why she would," San Ignacio said.
"I too find *Nort' Americanos* difficult to understand. Of
course, despite everything, I find I like your cousin,
Alison. He is an *hombre muy simpatico.*"

"Yes," Alison said in a depressed voice. "We could
have shaped him up very well."

San Ignacio, his masculinity affronted, objected. "You
should not speak of him so, Alison. And what about your
cousin Mrs. Webster and the proposition she is bringing?"

For a second a look of fright and doubt came over
Alison's face. Then she said firmly, "This is the time
when it is most important to remember that with God,
ALL things are possible. If we ever forget that we will
be in trouble. Where is Fat Buttery?"

Fat Buttery, once again naked, was sitting in the
middle of the floor tearing the last small piece of Mrs.
Daniels' letter to MacBain into even smaller pieces. He
was surrounded by what looked like a sea of confetti.

Alison and San Ignacio stared at the destruction.

"I wonder what was in it?" San Ignacio said.

"Probably nothing important. Fat Buttery, put on your
clothes."

5

Everyone expected the party of examining ladies to arrive that afternoon. But it was two days before they showed up.

In the meantime, MacBain, his foot in a cast and a crutch under his arm, had been driven back by Dr. Sharp.

"We had a letter for you from Mrs. Daniels. San Ignacio brought it," Alison said. "But Fat Buttery tore it up."

"Do you have any idea what was in it?" MacBain asked suspiciously, hobbling over to his chair in the corner of the kitchen.

"Well, sort of,"

"What does that mean?"

"Mrs. Daniels wrote a letter to me that I was reading to San Ignacio when Fat Buttery tore up yours. Maybe she said the same thing in yours as she did in ours."

"Which was? Don't keep me in suspense. It's bad for my ankle."

Alison eyed him warily. "Well, she said she told the Child Welfare officer that you were going to adopt us. Don't stamp your foot, Cousin Nicholas. That's your bad one."

MacBain closed his eyes until the pain subsided. Then he lowered himself into his chair. Alison watched him nervously. "May I get you something?" she asked.

MacBain opened his eyes. "What would you suggest?"

"Er—coffee?"

"How about hemlock?"

Alison's rather pinched little face lit up with a smile.

"Like Socrates? You know, sometimes you make me think of Daddy. Except, of course, he was a very good man."

"Thank you. Remind me not to ask you for any character reference. As you so chivalrously pointed out, your father was the good cousin who always wanted to be a medical missionary."

"And what did you always want to be?"

"What I am," MacBain snapped. "A writer."

This time Alison was wise enough to leave it at that.

During the next few days, Alison, San Ignacio and even Fat Buttery, determined to show MacBain how lucky he would be to have them live there.

"This house is gloomy," Alison told San Ignacio and Fat Buttery. "We're going to make it look cozy."

"Perhaps," San Ignacio said, "he doesn't wish it to look cozy. Perhaps gloom is better for writing books."

"He just *says* he's a writer."

"Do you know that he has *not* written a book?"

"I can't see any."

"That does not mean he has not done it."

"This male solidarity business is beginning to get on my nerves," Alison said crossly. "Anyway, we can at least make it clean."

So they dusted and polished and swept and scrubbed, while MacBain, after a sour look, hopped his way up to his study, which was in the attic on the other side of the house and where he had strictly forbidden anyone to follow him.

"It's off limits. Do you all understand that?"

"Yes, Cousin Nicholas," said the chorus of three.

"I'm not—oh, well, never mind," he said, and hopped out of sight.

That first night MacBain grudgingly told them that two more folding cots were in the small room off Alison's attic and they would also find sheets and blankets there. So after they had finished with the kitchen and the living room, they all trouped up.

The room contained not only two folding cots, but a cedar chest and lots of bookshelves filled with books.

"Here are all the Betsy Bounce books!" Alison cried in delight.

"They're just for girls," San Ignacio said loftily. Even so, he took a few down to look at them.

An hour later the three cots were all made up properly, some soft lights were on and the three were very quiet. Alison and San Ignacio were reading. Fat Buttery was sound asleep.

"Don't you want to eat?" MacBain bellowed into the silence some time later.

He had made a huge kettle of vegetable and noodle soup, with bread, cheese and salad.

"We meant to cook dinner for you," Alison said, conscience stricken. "But we got to reading. You have all the Betsy Bounce books."

MacBain, who was in the act of ladling out the soup, accidentally spilled some.

"We just washed the floor," Alison said sadly.

"You can see now why I don't like women around.

They're always claiming they just washed the floor or the clothes or whatever. Floors are to be spilled on."

Fat Buttery, who had been noisily drinking his soup, held his spoon at half mast for a thoughtful minute and then threw its contents at MacBain. "Nathty! Nathty to Alithon!" His face went red and he scowled.

"Never mind, Fat Buttery. He really has the right to spill on his own floor," Alison said.

MacBain looked at Fat Buttery for a minute, and then said grudgingly, "You're a good man, Peter John. You stick up for your friends. I applaud that."

The rest of the dinner passed without comment. Mac-Bain and San Ignacio did the dishes while Alison put Fat Buttery to bed and read him a Betsy Bounce book, the one about the badger who thought he was a rabbit.

On the third day, there was a knock at the front door, and when Alison went to answer it, four ladies stepped in. When Alison saw the first three, her heart sank. They all seemed to have gray hair, sharp noses and flowered hats. But the fourth lady was quite different. She was young, pretty, with a warm smile and brown eyes.

The tallest one with the sharpest nose said, "I'm Mrs. Sanders. These are Mrs. Johnson, Mrs. Sedgwick and Miss Grant. We're from the Civic Committee. And you must be Alison."

Alison had had vague plans of stalling the Ladies Committee because something told her that no good would come of this visit. But Mrs. Sanders was so over-whelming that before Alison knew what she was doing, she had opened the door wide and all four ladies were inside.

"Hmm," Mrs. Sanders said, looking around. She sniffed. "Well, at least it's clean."

"Needs curtains," the second lady said.

"I don't approve of bachelors taking care of children," the third lady said.

"Did you do this . . . all this really excellent cleaning?" Miss Grant asked, smiling at Alison.

Alison's face went red with pleasure. "All three of us did it."

"Where are the others?" Mrs. Sanders asked.

"I'll get them."

A few minutes later, the four ladies were seated in a

semi-circle and facing them, in another semi-circle, were Alison, San Ignacio and Fat Buttery.

"This is terribly formal," Miss Grant said. "Why don't we sit on the sofas? Alison and I can make tea. What about it, Alison?"

Alison thought it a splendid idea, so while the three ladies and two boys were rearranging themselves on the sofa and in the wing chairs in the living room, Alison and Miss Grant put on the kettle and got out the tea cups.

"Alison, while I'm making the tea, why don't you slip out to my car and look in the back? I brought some cakes and cookies because I thought it possible that you didn't have any."

"That's super of you, Miss Grant. I'll be right back." And she was, with two square boxes, the contents of which filled four plates.

"Now we can carry them in," Miss Grant said.

Alison, whose mind had suddenly been struck with a brilliant new possibility said, "You aren't married, are you? I mean, you are *Miss* Grant?"

"No. I'm not married. I'm the fifth grade teacher and I'm on the Civic Committee. Why do you ask?"

"I was wondering . . . " Alison rearranged a couple of little cakes and glanced quickly at Miss Grant. "You aren't *against* marriage, are you? You haven't taken a vow or anything?"

Miss Grant's mouth quivered toward a smile. "No. I haven't taken any vow. I just haven't found anybody I wanted to marry."

"But you're open to possibilities?" Alison pursued hopefully.

"What do you have in mind, Alison?"

"Cousin Nicholas. I'm sure he needs a wife, and it

would make things so much easier for us."

"What are you saying?" bellowed an outraged voice from the kitchen door. "How dare you ask somebody to marry me!"

MacBain limped over on his crutch. He glared at Miss Grant, who, to Alison's great admiration, did not look in the least frightened. In fact, she even looked as though she might be having a hard time not to laugh.

MacBain said, "I must tell you . . . please don't . . . that is . . . I don't wish to be rude, but . . ."

"Don't worry, Mr. MacBain," the pretty school teacher said. "I won't marry you. I promise."

MacBain looked like a man who didn't know whether to feel relieved or insulted. For want of anything else to do, he glared at Alison. "I'll speak to you later about this," he said in an ominous voice.

Alison was beginning to see that not all of her inspirations seemed, on the face of it, heaven sent, and it made her feel depressed.

"Please don't scold Alison," Miss Grant said. "She was only trying to be helpful."

"Do all those women believe that nonsense about my being Alison's long-lost father, the story that Alison— no doubt still trying to be helpful—told to Sanders, that puffed up bullfrog? Because I'm not. Alison is my cousin. That's all."

"And what about the other two? Is she related to them?"

MacBain glanced at Alison's anxious face. "She is their Earth Mother," he said.

"Their what?"

"You haven't read *The Golden Bough?* Tut!"

"Of course I've read *The Golden Bough!* Don't tell me those children have!"

"At their father's knee, along with what I am sure your good ladies will consider other unsuitable reading matter. Get Alison to tell you about it."

MacBain took a grip on his crutch and hopped to the kitchen door. "Very edifying," he said.

Miss Grant, following with the tea tray, looked in a puzzled way at Alison. "I thought you were all missionaries."

MacBain said over his shoulder, "It appears that some counter-conversion has been going on."

"It certainly does." By this time they were in the sitting room.

Alison said rather pompously, as she started to hand around the plates, "Truth is one; men call it variously."

"What did you say?" queried Mrs. Sanders, her nose pointing like a bird dog's.

Alison repeated it.

Mrs. Sanders' nose almost seemed to quiver. "And where did you get that?"

"Well, Father used to say it. But he said he got it from The Vedas—you know, the Hindu Scriptures."

From that point the tea party went down hill badly.

"I think it most strange that you quote some heathen outfit," Mrs. Sanders said, refusing cream, lemon or sugar.

San Ignacio fired up. "Hindus are not heathen. I am a Hindu. I should know."

"I thought you were a Christian," said the lady with the second sharpest nose.

"And according to my husband, the son of an Inca princess," Mrs. Sanders said.

MacBain, who had sat down on his most uncomfortable chair because it was the only one left and the one nearest the door, stared into his teacup. "They are not

mutually exclusive," he said finally, and shifted un-
easily. He was, by far, the tallest and biggest person in
the room, and the frail cane-bottomed chair was creak-
ing in protest.

Alison, who tended to be helpful even when she didn't
stop to think about it, said absent-mindedly, "Would you
like to change chairs with me, Cousin Nicholas? I think
mine is bigger than yours."

Mrs. Sanders zeroed in accusingly, "You told my
husband he was your long-lost father."

"Probably just a flight of wishful thinking," Miss Grant
hastily suggested, but to no effect. Mrs. Sanders knew a
wrongdoer when she saw one and brushed straight over
her.

"You are a wicked, untruthful, unChristian girl, and
it is obvious you need strict disciplining—away from all"
—her eye lit on MacBain—"unholy and"—her gaze
traveled to San Ignacio—"foreign influences."

Alison got up, knocking over a plate of fudge cookies,
several of which flew onto Mrs. Sanders' velvet lap.

"I am *not* untruthful and wicked and I *am* a Christian
and you are obviously just the kind of Christian my
father said did more harm than good."

"Hear, hear!" MacBain said, and added, "Right on."

Mrs. Sanders turned on him in righteous fury. "And
it is perfectly obvious to me that you are no fit person to
have charge of these misguided—"

"We are not misguided and you are an old witch-
doctor, an evil one," San Ignacio said, striding over to
her. "I shall recite a spell so that your tongue will refuse
to speak: *Ooomba ooomba . . .*"

Who knows what might have happened to Mrs.
Sanders' tongue if there had not been an interruption?

Fat Buttery, clothed in nothing but one of MacBain's neckties looped around his sturdy waist, erupted into the room. In his hand, resurrected from his suitcase, was his greatest treasure, a miniature Andean blowpipe. Uttering a yell, he started a war-dance, trampling the fudge cookies into the rug.

MacBain said one of his wicked words and started to laugh. Finishing his brief dance, Fat Buttery leaped onto MacBain's lap. The chair broke. MacBain, his plaster cast, the chair and Fat Buttery all landed on Mrs. Sanders' feet.

With a shriek she stood up. "This is nothing more than a bacchanal. I shall have the Child Welfare people in here by tomorrow morning. It is out of the question that you should be in charge of these children. You should never have offered to take in your cousin, if she is your cousin."

"I didn't and she is," MacBain growled from the floor where, with San Ignacio's help, he was trying to get up.

"And bad enough—though not as bad—that you should have the two boys. One of them should go to our Indian reservation."

"He's not that kind of Indian," MacBain said, struggling to his feet.

"And as for this—" she averted her eyes from Fat Buttery's naked form. She shuddered. "Disgraceful!"

MacBain brushed himself off. "He's dressed in the fashion of our noble ancestor, Adam, *before* he was expelled from Eden, and therefore still in Grace. I see no harm in it."

"That was before he ate the forbidden fruit."

"Which his companion, a woman of course, gave him."

Fat Buttery had been looking at Mrs. Sanders in a

speculative way. Suddenly he came to a conclusion. "Bad!" he yelled. "Bad," and hid his face with one hand while he pointed towards the enraged woman with the other. "Bad," he repeated sadly.

"I'm leaving," Mrs. Sanders said. "I'll have you know young man—"

There was a loud knock on the front door.

"Alison," MacBain said, "go see who's there and tell them we aren't in."

"Alison ran to the door and opened it. "We aren't in —oh, hello, Mrs. Daniels!" There was a pause. "And Cousins Pamela and Victoria, and Elaine." Enthusiasm decreased with each name.

A nice-looking elderly woman with gray hair, followed by a fashionably dressed woman with striped hair and two little girls about Alison's age, came in.

"My, you're having a party! How nice!" Mrs. Daniels said, kissing Alison. "Peter John, shouldn't you put some clothes on?"

"No," Fat Buttery said.

San Ignacio was making a low and courtly bow.

"Alison," her Cousin Pamela said, "we had a family conclave and came to the decision that we want you to come and live with us. Think of it! Won't that be nice?"

Alison had a terrible feeling, as though solid gold bars were being lowered around her. "San Ignacio? Fat Buttery?"

"Well, since they're boys and our cousin here has never done anything for anyone in his whole life, we also decided that he could take them for the time being."

"Oh, you did, did you?" MacBain said.

"Do you object? With all this room?"

"Of course I object. This is my home, and if you make

the slightest move to foist anyone on me, I'll sue you for
... for ... invasion of privacy."

"Selfish, selfish, selfish," Mrs. Webster said, smooth-
ing her gloves. "They'll simply have to go into an orphanage. When I think of these two poor homeless,
innocent—"

"Then why don't you take them?"

"I haven't room. You should know that. What with
Vicki and Percy and their friends."

"Then why don't you get rid of two of your maids and
one of your gardeners?"

"That's just the kind of prejudicial attitude ... " They
battled on. Alison, San Ignacio and Fat Buttery looked
horror struck. Even Miss Grant looked unhappy.

"Aren't you lucky?" Vicki said to Alison. "Now you
can come and live with us and learn about television and
boyfriends and school and everything. My friend Elaine,
here, and I belong to the best club at school, and if you're
good we'll let you join, but you'll have to do something
about your clothes."

"No. I won't," Alison cried. "I'd hate it. I'd much
rather go back to the headhunters. San Ignacio, Fat
Buttery ... " Fearfully she looked at them. After all, her
Cousin Nicholas had said that they could live with him.
But she needn't have worried.

"We'll not stay at all," San Ignacio said. He turned to
MacBain. "You are no longer my friend, not saying you
would take Alison."

"I didn't not say ... "

"We are leaving. Now. We will find a home together
somewhere. Goodbye."

And the three of them walked out of the living room
and out of the house, Alison and San Ignacio dressing

R

Fat Buttery as they went.

Everybody stared after them, too astonished to do anything.

"That's my tie they're taking," MacBain said. But he didn't look too unhappy.

"This is ridiculous," Mrs. Webster protested. "Three children can't simply walk out because they don't want to do what they're told."

"Why not?" MacBain asked. "Anyway, they're doing it."

"Somebody must stop them. Immediately!" She opened the living room window and leaned out. "Children! Come back here at once. I order you! This minute. Do you hear me?"

But by this time Alison and San Ignacio had managed to get Fat Buttery dressed. So they just took to their heels and ran. After a minute or so, they were out of sight, heading north, along the shore, into the trees.

"Isn't anyone going to go after them?" Mrs. Webster said. She looked around indignantly.

"Not with my cast," MacBain said.

Mrs. Sanders sniffed. Rapidly passing over the three elderly women, she turned to the young schoolteacher. "Miss Grant, I insist you pursue them."

Miss Grant sighed and put down her teacup. "All right. But you know, I think if we all just left things alone for a bit they'd work out."

"That's a lax doctrine I have never been able to bring myself to accept," Mrs. Sanders said.

"The whole village knows that," MacBain replied ungraciously.

She gave him an icy stare, then turned to the schoolteacher. "Miss Grant?"

Miss Grant went out the front door, ran lightly across the open turf to the circle of trees and disappeared. About forty minutes later she was back.

"Well, they've either outrun me or are hidden. I couldn't find a trace. I still think we should just wait and see. I have great faith that Alison will cope."

MacBain said, "I have a feeling you're right."

"Well!" Mrs. Sanders said, "since you're both obviously irresponsible, I shall take it upon myself to inform Officer Connors."

"That should make his day perfect," MacBain said gravely.

6

An hour or so later Alison and San Ignacio and Fat Buttery were still walking in and out of clumps of spruce and pine that ran parallel to the shore. For some time no one had said anything, although Fat Buttery was beginning to make grunting noises that meant he was tired. Furthermore, it was getting to be dusk and, since it was September, it was also getting cold.

Finally San Ignacio said, "Where are we going, Alison?"

That question had been thrusting itself at Alison for the past hour. But she said, "Away. Away from all those people who are trying to change us or separate us or tell us we're wicked."

This answer comforted them for a while. Then quite

abruptly, Fat Buttery sat down. "Tired," he said. "No more."

Alison and San Ignacio looked down at him. Then San Ignacio said, "He's right, Alison. I'm tired, too. And hungry. And I bet you are also. We can't go on. We have to live somewhere."

"They'll try to divide us."

There was another silence. Then San Ignacio said, "Do you think that woman can put me on an *American* Indian reservation?"

"Perhaps we could all live on a reservation," Alison suggested. But staring down at Fat Buttery's yellow curls she knew it wasn't true. Then she said firmly, "We should have prayer and meditation. That's exactly what Father would say."

"I'm too hungry," San Ignacio said.

"That's the best time. We'll sit here and meditate for guidance. Remember: with God, all things are possible. I should have remembered that much sooner. The moment we forget, things start to go wrong."

"It's very cold to meditate," San Ignacio said.

"Then we'll start with some hatha yoga. That will warm us up and stimulate our glands. Then we can meditate."

So they did the hare and the half-lotus and the fish and the cobra and the lion postures, then back in the full lotus.

"It occurs to me," San Ignacio said suddenly, "that if we went back to Cousin Nicholas's and succeeded in getting into the attic without his knowing, we could live there a long time with no one any wiser."

"You see, it works!" Alison said. "I was thinking something of the same. Let's go back."

It was dark by the time they had returned. San Ignacio

and Alison had been alternating carrying Fat Buttery piggy-back, and they were all very tired and very hungry.

They looked at the house from the edge of the nearest trees. Since it was fully lighted, it was hard to tell where MacBain might be.

"If it just had a fire escape we could go up and come down into the attic," San Ignacio said.

"Hungry," Fat Buttery cried. "*Muy* hungry."

"Shh!" Alison and San Ignacio shushed him.

"Since it's dark, we can just run across and look through the kitchen window. Maybe he's in there," Alison said.

The word kitchen made them think about food. It seemed an irresistible idea. Quietly, they ran across the open grass to the back of the house. Fortunately, the window ledges were low so at least Alison and San Ignacio could see above them.

"Ahhh!" They pressed their noses against the glass. Laid out on the kitchen table were half a cooked chicken, bread, cheese, milk, a big salad and the remains of the fudge cookies.

Frantic tugs on their clothes attracted their attention.

"Let me see! Let me see!" whispered Fat Buttery.

So they raised him up and all three gazed in.

"It's a pity I'm a vegetarian," San Ignacio said, looking at the chicken. "But there is enough for me, anyway."

"I'm not a vegetarian, nor is Fat Buttery," Alison said. "We can have the chicken, and you can have most of the salad. We'll divide the rest."

They waited. "Do you think it is a trap?" San Ignacio said. "I mean, they wait while we are eating, then they pounce?"

"We'll just have to risk it. There's no way we can get on the roof and come down. Let's see if the window will open."

It did. In less than a minute all three were in the kitchen.

They sat down and for a long time there was no sound at all except for contented eating.

After they were all full, San Ignacio said, "But Cousin Nicholas will know someone has eaten his food."

"If we clean it up, and make some more salad, and get out more bread and cheese, perhaps he won't notice. He'll just think he put the same amount out."

"What about the chicken? You and Juan Pedro ate it all."

"Perhaps he will just think he made a mistake, that he didn't put it out."

"You are foolish if you think a man does not know if he puts out a chicken for his dinner."

"Well, what else do you suggest?" Alison asked.

"We can see if there's another chicken. Perhaps he buys several at once. He is a big man. He would eat many chickens."

But they couldn't find the slightest sign of a chicken. So they buried the remains of the one they had eaten outside, washed all the dishes and knives and forks they had used, replenished as much as they could from the refrigerator and the larder, and left the table looking as nearly as possible the same as when they came in.

Then, taking off their shoes and tiptoeing through the swinging door, they crept soundlessly upstairs. Fat Buttery swung between them so that he would touch the floor as little as possible and the danger of sound could be reduced.

Once up in the attic they gave a sigh of relief. The

light up there was on, too. But they turned it off a few seconds later, pausing only long enough to get Fat Buttery partially undressed and tucked in. Then they flung off their outer clothes and sank into their cots. In another minute all three were asleep.

When Alison woke up the next morning, the sky through the skylight was a pale, pinkish gray, and she knew it was very early. Both San Ignacio and Fat Buttery were still asleep.

It was at this hour of the morning that she always held her imaginary conversations with her father, because in the North Indian mission compound where they lived, her father would wake her up while it was still dark and then would take her by the hand out of sight of the other bungalows and houses. Together they would watch the great red ball come up from behind the towering white peaks, the high spine of the world, as her father called the Himalayas. It was then they would have their conversations about God and people and yoga and school and anything else that occurred to them.

Alison turned on her side and stared at the skylight, going over some of the things her father had said, such as:

> With God, all things are possible.
> Never despair. *that way*
> Trust Him.
> Be practical at all times.
> Don't ever tell a lie; especially not to yourself.

But as she ran through these as though she were telling beads, she knew she was doing it partly as preventive medicine. If she was totally truthful with herself, she knew this could not go on. Her dream of finding a home where the three of them could live was becoming clouded. It had seemed so simple: Any obstacle was merely practical and could therefore be overcome. But the whole adult world, which was far more powerful and complicated than anything she had ever before encountered, was against it. They would be divided. They would be told exactly what to do. Nobody wanted anything they had to give. They had to be taken apart and made over before they could even be acceptable. I wish I were back in India or in Peru, Alison thought. She looked over at the other cots. San Ignacio, his black hair spread over the pillow and the top of the sheet, was hunched under the bedclothes. Fat Buttery was spread-eagled on his back, his golden eyelashes making half circles on his red cheeks. They were absolutely beautiful. Alison thought, and her growing certainty that if found by the adults San Ignacio would be taken away because he was brown, and Fat Buttery because he was young, was more than she could bear.

"With God," she said forcefully to herself, "ALL things are possible. I must remember that all the time, every minute." For good measure she sat up and said it again.

Then she got softly out of bed, dressed, very quietly lifted a chair under the skylight, put some books on that, and stood on top of the pile. Then she opened the skylight and hauled herself out on the roof. It was cold and beautiful. Sitting on the ridge at the top, with her arm around the chimney stack, she watched the pink streaks flush into rose and then into deep crimson. Then she watched the great red-gold sun lift out of the ocean.

She sat there for a long time, trying not to think of anything at all, just letting thoughts and pictures float through her mind and detaching herself from them as she had been taught. Most of the pictures seemed to be of her father and Cousin Nicholas. They came and went and chased each other. After a while there were no thoughts at all. Just the sun and herself. A long time later, when she was quite cold and at peace, she came down into the attic.

Alison found San Ignacio and Fat Buttery awake when she stepped down off the chair beneath the skylight. San Ignacio's bed was neatly made and he was sitting cross-legged in the middle of it. Fat Buttery's bed looked as though it had been hit by a typhoon, the blankets and sheets ripped off, whirled into a knot and thrown back in the middle of the bed. Fat Buttery, one of his blankets held round his shoulders and trailing behind him like a cloak, jogged around the room singing a strange assortment of syllables.

"What is he doing a spell for?" Alison asked San Ignacio.

"For breakfast. He's hungry. So am I. Where have you been?"

"On the roof. Meditating. Why don't you try it? The sky's beautiful."

"I'm too hungry, and it's no use telling me that's the best time for meditating, because with me it's not true. If I am hungry that is all I can think of."

Suddenly Fat Buttery stopped. "Hungry!" he said loudly.

"Shhhh!" Both Alison and San Ignacio hissed. "Cousin Nicholas will hear us."

Fat Buttery hesitated for a moment and then sat down in the middle of the room. "Hungry," he said softly, his hands around his well padded stomach. "Hungry, Alithon."

"Yes, I know, Fat Buttery. We're all hungry. We'll have breakfast soon."

"How?" San Ignacio asked. "Just go to your cousin

and say 'we give ourselves up?' All these people will come and take us away."

Fat Buttery started to cry.

"I'll go down when Cousin Nicholas has finished breakfast. You know he eats early and then maybe he'll go out."

"With his foot? Alison, you are not thinking," San Ignacio said scornfully.

"Well at least I'm *trying* to think. All you do is talk about being hungry."

"It's on my mind. Besides, men need more food than women."

"Yeth," Fat Buttery said. "More."

"Who told you that? It's silly!"

"No one needed to tell me. There are some things you just know."

"Well, I don't."

San Ignacio sat in moody silence while Alison made her own and Fat Buttery's bed.

"All right," she said. "I'll go down now and see if the coast is clear."

"We'll all go." San Ignacio got up and pulled Fat Buttery up. "We must be very, very quiet."

They took off their shoes and crept down the stairs. There wasn't a sound in the house. At the first landing they waited, scarcely breathing. Then, after hearing nothing, they tiptoed down to the ground floor, along the passage, and peered into the kitchen through the swing door.

It was empty. But the table wasn't. On it, like the night before, there were all kinds of food—bread, butter, a pitcher that almost certainly contained milk, a jar of honey and another of strawberry jam, fruit, and eggs sitting up in egg cups.

"I wonder if he's left," Alison said thoughtfully. But she was talking to air. San Ignacio and Fat Buttery were already sitting at the table, buttering bread and pouring milk.

Alison wasn't far behind. Nevertheless she said rather severely, "I think we should all practice mind over matter," but the last word emerged a little muffled, through a piece of bread.

There was a long, contented silence. When everybody was full, San Ignacio said, "Your cousin left the food for us, just as he did last night. Therefore he must know we are her. But why—if he does not wish to see us or have us here?"

"I don't know. I've been wondering myself."

"Perhaps he does not want anyone to know that he knows," San Ignacio said after a while. "Perhaps he is not so bad after all. Perhaps he doesn't want to give us away."

"Then why doesn't he tell us?" Alison asked.

San Ignacio thought for a bit. "If he says he doesn't know where we are then, pouf! a little while later they find out he does, they will send him to jail."

Alison thought about it. "That doesn't sound much as though he were going to adopt us, does it?"

"It's too bad," San Ignacio said, "that he doesn't like women."

"He doesn't like children, either, remember? I think we'd better wash up."

They washed and dried the dishes and cutlery and put everything away.

San Ignacio looked out the window wistfully. It was a beautiful day in early autumn. Thrusting up the window he leaned out and breathed deeply. "I would like to run and run and run."

"Well, you can't. Somebody might see you."

"Run," Fat Buttery said, and before they could stop him he had, through the kitchen door, leaving his clothes on the floor behind him.

Alison and San Ignacio took off after the pinkly naked Fat Buttery across a wide area of turf, catching him in the grove of pines and bringing him back between them. It was then that they saw the police car. It was parked at the front door.

"Look!" San Ignacio said, pointing.

At that moment a police officer emerged from the front door with MacBain.

"He must be looking for us," Alison whispered.

"I bet that woman with the long nose sent him," San Ignacio said indignantly.

They stood at the edge of the grove, watching, as the officer shook hands with MacBain. MacBain said something. Then the officer laughed and started to the car. Just before he got in, he turned swiftly towards the grove. Alison and San Ignacio plunged down behind a low bush, dragging Fat Buttery down with them and holding their hands over his mouth to prevent him from giving their would-be captor a friendly cheer.

"Hush! Fat Buttery," Alison murmured. "We don't want him to know we're here."

"Do you think he saw us?" San Ignacio asked anxiously.

Alison watched the officer turn back to the car and wave to MacBain. There was a big grin on his face. Then he got in the car and drove off. MacBain, after a glance towards the trees, went back into the house, slamming the door rather loudly behind him.

"I don't know," Alison said doubtfully.

"If Cousin Nicholas knows we are here, wouldn't he tell the policeman?"

"Yes. At least he might. But then why wouldn't the policeman take us away?"

They contemplated this puzzle in silence while they waited till the coast was clear, then they went back to the house, Fat Buttery between them, quietly but vigorously protesting his capture.

After they got him dressed, San Ignacio, who was already thinking about lunch, said, "Why don't we make some sandwiches and take them upstairs?"

"That's a good idea," Alison said.

So they made some ham and cheese and some tomato and cheese and some plain cheese sandwiches, wrapped them in foil and took them back up to the attic.

San Ignacio scowled, "Now what do we do?"

"I'll read you a Betsy Bounce book," Alison promised, going into the little room where the books were.

"I think it is *muy* strange that a man like Cousin Nicholas has Betsy Bounce books in his attic."

"I don't see why," Alison protested, loyal to her favorite author. "Betsy Bounce books are for *everyone.*"

So for the next hour or two she read what happened to Chippingdale Worthington, the chipmunk, who decided to carve a career for himself in the city, but who found that there was too much prejudice in the city against people with bushy tails and on the last page returned happily to his cottage in the country.

"That was good," San Ignacio said, forgetting that since he was almost a man he considered himself above such childish stories.

"Yes," Alison said.

"Other one," Fat Buttery said. "More."

"Why don't we play a game?" Alison suggested. Her voice was tired. "Then we could read another one after lunch."

At the magic word San Ignacio and Fat Buttery glanced towards the sandwiches on the table.

"Perhaps a little taste—" San Ignacio started.

"No," Alison said. "Later. Let's play 'I spy.' "

So they played "I spy."

Then they played seeing if they could get around the room on top of the furniture without touching the floor. They jumped and stretched and hopped from bed to chest to bed to table to bed to bureau and back again. Alison and San Ignacio managed quite well. But Fat Buttery bounced on the floor several times, making loud thumps but suffering little damage. Then they did yoga breathing and exercises for about forty-five minutes.

Then they had lunch and a nap.

San Ignacio and Fat Buttery went to sleep almost immediately, but Alison lay awake for a while wondering what was going to happen to them and how long her cousin was going to play this game of hide-and-seek and how soon his patience would give out. Then she finally went to sleep.

When they woke up, San Ignacio was hungry again.

"What I would like most," San Ignacio said, "is some tortillas."

"Think about something else," Alison suggested.

"No. I wish to think about tortillas."

"I'll read you another book."

"This time," San Ignacio said, "I will read aloud. Your voice will get tired."

So he read Betsy Bounce's book about Harry the Hedgehog, who had to go on a diet before he could become an airline pilot. San Ignacio picked that out from the shelf of Betsy Bounce books in the closet because he himself wanted to become a pilot.

Then, when they were sure Cousin Nicholas had finished dinner, they went down to find a big pot of hot meat and vegetable stew on the stove, with bread and salad and cheese and milk. After dinner, because it was dark, they went out for a walk. There was a half moon shining brightly, so they also treated themselves to some races across the grass beside the house, a few handstands, a vigorous game of tag, another race and another game of tag. At that point Fat Buttery sat down and in two seconds went to sleep.

"Here, Fat Buttery, you'll get cold," Alison said, hauling him onto her lap and putting her arms around him. Then San Ignacio wrapped his blanket around all three of them.

"That's funny," Alison said suddenly.

"What?" San Ignacio said drowsily. Chilly as it was, he was about to follow Fat Buttery's lead.

"I saw Cousin Nicholas in the window up there. He was watching us."

"Where?"

"He's gone now, but it was that window over the big one below."

"Where's his study?"

Alison thought. "Well, it's in the other part of the house, behind our attic. I saw it once when I was exploring. You can't see it from here."

"Are you sure you saw him?"

"Positive. I think it's his bedroom."

"I suppose," San Ignacio said after a while, "it is because he wants to keep this house that he hasn't told on us. That man, the silly one who calls us innocent and helpless, said that if he didn't keep us the bank would make him leave."

Alison tried to envision anyone making her difficult cousin do what he didn't want to do.

"Maybe," she said cautiously.

After that they went back up to the attic and went to bed.

It was the following day that MacBain's motive for keeping out of sight became clear.

Alison, San Ignacio and Fat Buttery had just had their sandwiches for lunch when there was the sound of a car driving up to the house. All three heads poked out of the dormer window.

"That's the Websters' car," Alison said. Her heart was beginning to beat faster. Even though she didn't really think Cousin Nicholas would give away their hiding place, she was frightened. And she could tell by the way San Ignacio and Fat Buttery were pressing against her, not making a sound, that they were frightened, too.

Then Mrs. Webster got out of the car, followed by Mrs. Daniels and Mr. Sanders. Mrs. Webster knocked at the door.

In a minute MacBain appeared through the front door. Alison and the others couldn't hear what Mrs. Webster said, but they could hear MacBain's reply quite clearly.

"I haven't seen them."

In fact, he seemed to be speaking even more loudly than usual.

"There's no need to shout," Mrs. Webster said.

"I just wanted to be sure you heard that I haven't had a word with them."

"Disgraceful! Unbelievable!" Mr. Sanders said. "Those innocent, helpless—"

"Alison is not in the least helpless," Mrs. Daniels said. "Nor is San Ignacio."

"—wandering around the countryside," Mr. Sanders went on as though no one had said anything. "The bank will take a very serious view of this, MacBain. I told you that if you did not at least offer a shelter to those sweet young creatures—"

"I've been talking to my lawyer," MacBain said. "You can't evict me. It's against the law. I haven't done any harm to the house—in fact I've had repairs done that you were too stingy to make. I haven't disturbed any neighbors. How could I? I don't have any. And besides, I'm a writer—"

"Ha!" Mr. Sanders snorted.

"—and I've paid my rent on time and regularly."

"It is the suspicious *origins* of your income—"

"—which are none of your business."

"The bank feels—"

MacBain said something extremely rude about the bank.

"If that's going to be your attitude," Mr. Sanders said in a deep huff, "I shall have no more to say to you."

"May I count on that?"

Mr. Sanders stumped off and got into the car. "Come, ladies," he said. "There is no further point in discussing anything with anyone so . . . so—" He was still groping for the right word as they drove off.

Upstairs the three heads pulled away from the window.

"If it's true what he says about it being against the law," San Ignacio said, "then he will not have to keep us here. He will tell them where we are."

"Yes," Alison agreed. "But then why didn't he tell them right away?"

They pondered over this and could find no answer. "You didn't eat your lunch, Alison" San Ignacio said suddenly. "Here is a whole sandwich and another half."

"I wasn't hungry."

"And you didn't eat much breakfast."

Alison didn't say anything. There was a nasty tight feeling in her middle. "Why don't I read you a Betsy Bounce story?"

So she read the story about the dolphin who could not only talk and read and write, but who held swimming classes for children and led them all to a magic cave on the bed of the ocean. This was one of Alison's and San Ignacio's favorites, so they didn't notice at first that Fat Buttery was trying to make a boat with a piece of paper until the crackling disturbed them.

"Fat Buttery, what are you doing? You're supposed to listen while I read. You know you like Betsy Bounce."

"Boat," Fat Buttery said. "Nice boat."

"That's the wrong way to make it," San Ignacio reached over and pried the paper loose. Fat Buttery uttered a wail.

"Shhhh!" his elders said.

"BOAT!" Fat Buttery cried desolately.

"All right! I'll just show you how to make it."

San Ignacio smoothed the paper and looked at what was on it. "It's a letter to your Cousin Nicholas."

"You shouldn't read somebody else's mail," Alison said, craning over his shoulder to see what was written on it. "Fat Buttery, where did you get this?"

"Book," Fat Buttery said. "In book. Fall out. Make boat now."

"In a minute."

There was a short silence. Then San Ignacio said, "Read it aloud, Alison. I don't know all the words."

So Alison read:

> *Dear Mr. MacBain:*
> *Enclosed is the advance we discussed for your next*
> *three books written under the pseudonym of Betsy*
> *Bounce. The Betsy Bounce series has proved enor-*
> *mously popular, and we look forward to many more*
> *titles.*
>
> > *Yours truly,*
> >
> > *James Waldo Entwistle*
> > *Editor*

At the bottom of the letter were the words, *Enclosed:*
check for followed by a dollar sign and a large figure.

"What's a peeseudonym?" San Ignacio asked.

"I think it's a name you use if you don't want to use
your own. Sort of a pen name," Alison said in a dazed
voice. "Only I don't think you pronounce the 'p'."

After a minute San Ignacio said unbelievingly,
"Cousin Nicholas is Betsy Bounce?"

They stared at one another for a moment. Then San
Ignacio gave a whoop and jumped up. "COUSIN NICH-
OLAS IS BETSY BOUNCE!" he yelled.

7

Alison was still looking stunned, but as San Ignacio gave another whoop, her worried face broke into a smile.

"Do you know what this means, Alison?"

"It means that he is *very* talented. They're my favorite books."

"It also means that is where he gets his money. And Alison—"

She had been reading the letter again, but she looked up. "Yes?"

"If he had wanted anyone to know about the books, he would have told that man from the bank and everyone else. But he is ashamed that he writes such children's books, a *muy hombre* like that. THEREFORE we can blackmail him."

"Yes," Alison said unenthusiastically.

"Why are you saying yes like that, as though it were a bad idea?"

"I want him to *want* us."

"Bah! What is important is that we will now have a home."

"I think we should meditate," Alison said. "We have been forgetting that with God, all things are possible. I am not sure that that includes blackmail."

"Very well. But I think it is just like a woman to find silly objections when we have hit on a really good idea."

"*You* have. Not we."

"Well I bet Fat Buttery thinks it's all right, don't you, Fat Buttery?"

Fat Buttery's eyes were swimming in tears. "Boat," he said miserably.

"All right. You can make your boat. But don't lose it or tear it," Alison said, handing over the letter.

San Ignacio was outraged. "That's our evidence."

"Fat Buttery will take care of it, won't you?"

"Yeth," Fat Buttery nodded, his fingers folding and refolding the letter.

Alison said, "I think we should start our meditation by saying aloud together, WITH GOD, ALL THINGS ARE POSSIBLE."

"Oh, all right," San Ignacio said rather crossly.

After they made their statement in chorus, Alison and San Ignacio sat in the lotus position, and Fat Buttery, in no particular position, quietly and happily went on with his boat.

After the meditation they had a nap and after the nap

they held a council of war. Alison finally agreed they would go down while MacBain was having his dinner and tell him they knew his dreadful secret.

"But I still don't think it's a good idea," she said. The vote had gone against her since Fat Buttery, who thought the plan would get them down to the kitchen and the accessibility of food, had voted with San Ignacio.

Accordingly, after they had all washed and brushed in the small bathroom outside their attic, they trooped downstairs about two hours earlier than usual.

MacBain was sitting at the kitchen table eating his dinner. He looked at them sternly as they filed in.

"How can I go on saying I haven't seen you when you come tramping in while I'm having my dinner? Go away."

Knowing that San Ignacio was bursting to launch his career in crime, Alison said hastily, "Well, if you don't want us, Cousin Nicholas, then why don't you tell Mr. Sanders and the others we're here and let them take us away—and divide us up?"

MacBain scowled. "I told you. That old billy goat banker is trying to blackmail me into making this some kind of orphanage by saying he will evict me."

"But we heard you tell him that your lawyer said he couldn't."

"I said that to keep him off the subject of innocent helpless children—which you aren't. What are you doing?"

This last was addressed to Fat Buttery who was climbing into his lap the better to reach the remains of a roast chicken.

"Chuck-chuck," Fat Buttery said, arm outspread, his stomach lying across MacBain's plate.

"That's what he calls a chicken," Alison informed her cousin.

"I can see that for myself. Here!" Detaching a wing, he handed it to Fat Buttery, who made himself comfortable on MacBain's lap and gave himself up to enjoyment, looking rather like a miniature Henry VIII.

"I didn't say you could stay here," MacBain said.

Fat Buttery, his mouth ringed with bits of chicken, gazed questioningly into MacBain's face and then produced one of his blinding, high-voltage smiles.

"Oh, all right," MacBain mumbled.

Alison found herself wishing, just for a second, that she could be where Fat Buttery was, taming the savage beast and being accepted by him, however reluctantly. But then she reproached herself for being, as the missionaries would have said, self-centered, and she reminded herself how lucky she and San Ignacio were to have Fat Buttery's charm winning the day where force and guile and even crime . . . but she had congratulated herself too soon.

"Speaking of blackmail," San Ignacio began ominously.

MacBain had been watching Alison's face from under his eyelids while he helped Fat Buttery detach one bone from another. He looked at San Ignacio. "Whose blackmail?"

San Ignacio drew a breath. "Ours. We know you're Betsy Bounce. A letter fell out of the book we were reading. You would not wish anyone to know that a man with such *machismo* writes such foolish children's books, would you?"

"They are not foolish," Alison said hotly. "They're marvelous. And I notice you listen just as much as anybody when they're being read."

"That is not the point," San Ignacio said hastily.

MacBain's cheeks had gone red above his beard. "What is this nonsense?" he roared, quite like his old self.

"It is not nonsense. We have the letter. Alison, you must have it." San Ignacio turned towards her.

"No, I don't. Fat Buttery had it. It's upstairs."

San Ignacio made an exclamation, then ran towards the door.

"So," MacBain said, "you have resorted to blackmail. And I suppose you're in on it."

"Yes," Alison said miserably. It had always been a rule that though they might disagree in private, they stuck together in public.

"I'm surprised at you."

San Ignacio's footsteps came pounding down the stairs and into the kitchen.

"I told you not to let him have it," he said furiously, forgetting they were not alone. "Now look!" He held up a soggy mass of paper.

Fat Buttery's arms reached out for it. "BOAT!" he yelled ecstatically.

"Well, so much for your evidence," MacBain said. "Thank you, Fat Buttery."

At that moment there was a knock on the front door.

"Probably," MacBain said, unloading Fat Buttery, "those will be some of our relatives, Alison, plus that meddling Sanders. Before you came I lived a quiet, untrammeled life. I didn't have callers more than once a year."

Alison was far too unhappy to reply, but San Ignacio called after him, "Remember! Even if we do not have the letter, we can tell!"

In a few minutes MacBain came back, followed by

✝ Mrs. Webster, Mrs. Daniels, Miss Grant and Mr. and Mrs. Sanders.

"Mrs. Daniels!" Alison, San Ignacio and Fat Buttery all cried at once and ran over to greet her. Then they greeted Miss Grant with almost equal affection, Alison because she liked her, San Ignacio because he thought she was pretty, and Fat Buttery because she picked him up and hugged him.

"Oh, what a sturdy boy!" she said. He crowed with delight and hugged her around the neck.

"He shouldn't be up at this hour," Mrs. Sanders said. "You are all wicked, thoughtless children running away like that worrying us all."

"I don't think you were a bit worried," Alison objected. "And anyway, how did you know we were here? I suppose that policeman told you."

"Yes, he did." Mrs. Sanders' narrow bosom heaved with indignation. "And he had the impertinence to suggest we leave you here." Her indignant eye went from MacBain to Miss Grant. "Someone," she said ominously, "must have gotten to him."

Miss Grant smiled at Alison. "I did. I told him I thought if . . . if everything quieted down I was sure things would come out all right."

Alison returned Miss Grant's smile. Then she said to Mrs. Sanders, "That's what I thought. You weren't worried at all. You were just mad."

"Now, now," Mr. Sanders put in hurriedly, an eye on the gathering storm. "Little ladies mustn't ever be rude or forget—"

"You are a silly old rooster," San Ignacio said, forgetting his previous plans. "You do not know anything.

Cousin Nicholas said you were a billy goat and he is right."

The banker went bright red. "How dare you, MacBain! I give you final warning. Either you take these—"

"Sweet, innocent children?" Mac Bain queried. "That was the way you described them, wasn't it?"

Mrs. Sanders' gloomy face looked even more sour. "I'm not sure Mr. MacBain is the right influence for these wicked, disobedient children."

"They're not wicked and disobedient," Mrs. Daniels said indignantly. "They're very good children, and a great help if you just treat them as sensible human beings. I don't know what we would have done without Alison at the mission. She cooked, she helped at the clinic, she taught Sunday School, she looked after San Ignacio and Peter John. She's a good girl."

"Then why don't you adopt her?" Mrs. Sanders said.

"Because I'm going to live with my daughter, which would be terrible if it weren't for my grandchildren. Besides, Alison wants to live here, don't you, dear?"

Alison nodded. She had become convinced that though MacBain might be induced to take the boys, he would not take her. It made her feel worse than anything had since her father had died. She looked for a minute at San Ignacio and Fat Buttery.

"Would you let San Ignacio and Fat Buttery stay here if I went back to New York?" she asked MacBain.

Her cousin was scowling so much his eyebrows were almost over his eyes.

"I haven't said I'd take anyone yet," he growled.

San Ignacio turned on him. "Well, I will tell them your secret. And Alison, how could you ask that? We stick together. We will not stay here or anywhere without you."

"Bravo!" Miss Grant said.

San Ignacio blushed, but since his cheeks were dark brown it didn't show.

"What secret?" Mrs. Sanders looked more pleased than anyone could remember seeing her. Her nose twitched.

San Ignacio drew a breath. "Cousin Nicholas is—"

"No," Alison said. "You mustn't, San Ignacio. That's not right."

"Here I have a scheme so that Cousin Nicholas will be forced to let us live here, and you say it's not right!"

"San Ignacio," the banker told him. "It is your duty to tell anything discreditable you may know about Mr. MacBain."

"Oh, no, it isn't," Mrs. Daniels said. "No one should be forced to do anything they don't want to do. And they shouldn't tattle, either!"

Mrs. Sanders was horrified. "Why—society would fall apart!"

"Rubbish!" Miss Grant said.

MacBain spoke up. "It's not really such a dreadful secret. Only San Ignacio thinks it shows me lacking in *machismo*. I'm the author of the Betsy Bounce books." He paused as there was a gasp from Miss Grant. "Yes?"

"Just surprise." Her eyes started to crinkle in a smile. "Do you know they're among the most popular books in the school library? Youngsters love them. They must sell in the thousands!"

"Just so," MacBain said. And they both laughed. He continued. "I started the first one as a joke when I was bored stiff working at your bank, Sanders. It sold immediately. So I wrote another one. That was twenty-one books ago. That, incidentally, is where I get the money you find so suspicious. The other day you referred sarcastically to the day I said I was in Boston. Well—I *was* in Boston, having lunch with my editor, who wanted to meet me. That was why you deliberately chose that day for that dismal, made-up, non-existant embezzlement."

"Well, if you insist your visit to Boston, for which you did not have the bank's permission—I beg your pardon?"

"I said 'Bah!'"

"That's what I thought you said, and I may add I do not approve of your attitude—" As MacBain seemed about to speak again, Mr. Sanders hurried on, "A visit for which, I repeat, you did not have the bank's permission, then why wouldn't you tell me why you were in Boston?"

"Because, like San Ignacio, I felt that to be the author of the Betsy Bounce books lacked *machismo*. I was younger then and more easily embarassed. And besides, I soon found out that that so-called embezzlement was caused by a hiccup in that over-sized computer you insisted on installing in your under-sized bank. You knew it, everyone else knew it, but you didn't want to admit it because that monster machine was your bright idea. And now that some large bank is showing interest in buying you out, you're trying to get rid of me so you can imply that old deficit is my fault."

Mr. Sanders made some not very convincing blustering noises.

"Wilbur!" Mrs. Sanders said. "I told you God made pens before he made computers. You just had to show off."

┼ "Quill pens and high stools," Miss Grant murmured.

"It is useless to continue this conversation," Mr. Sanders said, trying to get control of the situation back in his hands.

"Yes, it is," MacBain agreed. "Let's shake hands and call it a day. The children have to go to bed."

"You mean you're keeping them?"

"Now that I seem to be allowed to have some say in the matter, yes."

Even Mrs. Sanders looked less sour, thinking, no doubt, of what she would be saying to her husband when she got him alone.

"That's wonderful!" Miss Grant hugged all three and emerged with a sticky face since Fat Buttery, finding the conversation dull, had embarked on bread and honey.

"Well, goodbye, Alison." Mrs. Webster tried not to look too happy. "I'm sorry you won't live with us."

"No you aren't, Cousin Pamela," Alison said bravely. "You're just as glad as I am."

Mrs. Daniels hugged Alison, San Ignacio and Fat Buttery. "I'm so glad! Come and see me sometimes."

Then they all left.

"Thank you, Cousin Nicholas," San Ignacio said. "You will like living with us, you'll see."

"I'm sure I will," MacBain said dryly. "And my first duty is to point out to you that blackmail is not generally considered a socially acceptable way of getting what you want."

"No," San Ignacio acknowledged. "I can see now. It was not a good idea. I am sorry."

"Just a friendly hint. No, Fat Buttery, not on my trousers." Fat Buttery, sticky hands outspread, abandoned his attempt to embrace MacBain's leg.

"Go to bed, all of you. Since I am now going to be a father, I will need plenty of rest."

The two boys trooped out of the kitchen. Alison remained, looking at her cousin.

"Thank you very much, Cousin Nicholas. I know you'd rather have had the boys alone. I'll try not to get in the way."

MacBain sat down in his armchair, which still remained in the kitchen and was now near the range. "Come here."

Alison approached. Reaching out, MacBain pulled her gently onto his lap. "Now where, cousin, did you get that idea?"

The pinched look left Alison's face and her golden eyes started to shine. "But you said you didn't like women."

"So I did. Well, there're always exceptions. Now tell me about your working in the clinic and looking after babies and teaching Sunday School and running from cannibals. You seem to have led a very interesting life."

No one had ever said that to Alison and it cheered her enormously. So she told him everything, right from the beginning. By the time she finished she was relaxed, half leaning against MacBain's broad chest, drowsy in the heat from the grate.

"And then we came to New York," she finished.

"Well, well. No wonder you're such a little manager. But you mustn't try to manage me." Cupping her face he turned it around to face him. "Promise?"

She smiled. "I promise. Truly. But if—just out of habit—I start, you remind me."

"Don't worry. I will. That being the bargain, I think we'll do very well. You know, Alison, when you're

happy, you're a very pretty child." He kissed her. "Now go to bed." She gave him a hug and ran off to the stairs.

"Pretty," she said to herself. No one had ever called her that.

"Pretty is as pretty does," Mrs. Daniels had always stated.

Still, it was nice to be called pretty. Very nice.

Alison went quickly up the stairs to the attic to make sure Fat Buttery had washed his sticky hands before getting into bed.